THE GREEDY PRESIDENT

By
Kweku Nti Asare

**REDLAY PUBLICATIONS
GHANA, W/A**

kwakuntimasare@gmail.com

ISBN: 978-9988-54-223-8

Characters in this book are fictitious and they do not represent any person living or dead.

Life is like a relay race; we today, are but only participants in the race. Our concerted effort today, is what will determine the position of our posterity.

Prologue

People's Man watched the glassful of Akpeteshie for a while before he picked the drink and tossed it into his mouth. The usual sighing and face making followed, then he took his roll of marijuana from Oga, paid him – Oga was not crediting him anymore - and took a seat to smoke. He was smoking and was travelling in his head, thinking of how to survive the day when Gordon his roommate came in running to him.

"People's Man soldiers are looking for you run!" he said, panting.

"What have I done?" People's Man asked.

"I don't know they are all around."

1

By the time he entered the 'Pentagon' it was 16:17 hrs. The sun was going down, gradually loosing its grip on the city. The evening breeze was rightly exhibiting its coolness, bringing relief and comfort as it passed by. Occasionally, as if reminding everyone of its presence, 'the disgrace of the city'- whose waters were highly warm and humid at this time of the day - gave off its strong stench which stank noses as the breeze drove along, the only discomfort it carried. The regular din of the city which has been forgotten and hushed in the mind as people hustle and bustle about seeking daily goals, has got a new add up.

And since this new add up only pops up every four years, it always stands out when it emerges, overshadowing the daily noises of the city which have become part of the people that they did not even hear them, let alone recognize them and the new add up walks boldly among these daily noises as if it were a new noise in a silent place.

It was the year of elections and political machinery was at work. Party cars drove by with huge speakers mounted on them blasting off party songs and party messages. Numerous posters and paraphernalia even gained recognition above daily city activities and political arguments were rampant in every corner, sometimes heating up to a frenzy to gain yet another attention. The news was full of politics, conversations were full of politics, there was a sharp line of division amongst people and everyone stuck to his ideas and beliefs at this time.

This year's elections were exhibiting some uncertainties and many were predicting miracles and new happenings as new, strong and powerful people showed up and they were gaining the confidence of Ghanaians.

"Oga APC."

"Raw or bitters" Oga asked

"Raw."

"People's Man, you are owing me pay me before I give you anything," Oga demanded when he raised his eyes and saw who was standing before him.

"Oh Oga Molu, I will settle all my debt before day break I promise. Please you give me APC, APC two and give me two rolls. By nine o'clock when I finish campaigning, I will come and settle my bills," People's Man pleaded.

"And who is giving you that money to settle that bill?" Oga questioned.

"Oga," People's Man craned his neck closer to the counter and lowered his voice, "some people like what I am doing oo," he said. "You will see, you give me some, we shall talk later."

"Oh 'yate abrɛ'," Oga intoned. "This is what they do all the time. When they want the power, they recognize everybody whether the person is rich or poor, even the street boy becomes important. But afterwards, what do you see? They ride in their big cars wearing big coats and ties and ignore you, leaving you to your predicaments. How long would you learn?" he asked.

"Make hay while the sun shines Oga. We hit them while they are hot so don't worry," People's Man replied.

Oga Molu was still whining yet he positioned a glass and started pouring Akpeteshie into it. He pushed the glassful of liquor forward and People's Man grabbed it. He dipped a hand into a container and placed two rolls of marijuana on the counter as well.

"I will take the second APC when I'm leaving," People's Man said.

Oga turned to another customer. Beyond a partition people cheered suddenly. They were enjoying the afternoon movies. People's Man gulped down the hot Akpeteshie which changed the look on his face for a while. He then grabbed his two rolls of marijuana and left the counter for one of the benches that occupied the bar. He wrapped one of the marijuana into a roll and borrowed matches from a man sitting next to him. He lighted his weed, inhaled deeply and pulled himself into position.

When he started campaigning, he never thought he would get attention but it looked as if he had been wrong. Ghanaians were fed up just like him and people were listening to him. Feedback was good. One or two big men have started giving him 'chop' money and just this morning, a shop owner had bought him a megaphone. Things were going on. He, with the hand of God was going to bring these people down. He was doing all these not because of gain but for spiritual satisfaction. This was not stomach politics like the rest do but to People's Man, he was doing all he could as a good and devoted citizen of Ghana, hoping that one day he would see his country's liberation from evil, selfish and greedy men who had plummeted the country into poverty, stealing every money their hands could lay on with no regard for the welfare of the citizenry, who have become chocked and starving in the midst of plenty. It's his desire that one day, his country would belong to and become one of the nations who through prudent management of their resources have lifted the standard of living of their citizens with the youth and posterity having hope and confidence. A better future for everyone in the country.

He had finished high school, but coming from an underprivileged home, he had not been able to go to the university or any tertiary institution. So that was the end. He had to begin the struggle at an early age, first helping his family with the farm, but after some time People's Man - still his spirit fighting to see a better future - had opted to travel to the city, hoping things could be brighter there. Soon he had dropped in Accra to find out that jobs were not available. That meant absolutely no hope for people like him who accounted for thousands and those behind him who were even more. He had to resign to his fate and accepting the challenge, he had joined the many like him and settled in the slumps, suddenly becoming a ghetto boy who had to hustle for a living. Sometimes thinking about it, he did not know whether it was good he did not go to the university to waste scanty money and time or it was good he remained in his current situation. Neither was better than the other. They were all struggling, graduates and non graduates alike.

How could the youths of a country, people who naturally were growing to take over become so frustrated? No hope, no future. And what kicked him in the groin was the fact that it was not because the country was poor or something but as rich and favorably endowed as Ghana was, leaders in government could not do anything better for the country. He did not know whether it was because of ineptitude, foolishness, greed or whatever or just that they don't care. You see them every day in plushy cars, putting up mansions, their families getting better and better while the rest of the populace suffered. As for him, he had decided that it was because Ghanaian leaders were wicked and selfish. They just do not care and as a people they could not sit back and watch this happen in an era of democracy when it was they the people who chose these leaders into power.

Somehow Ghanaians must be blamed for their own sufferings because gone are the days when individuals usurped power and ruled the way they liked. Leaders were now chosen by the people. But People's Man wondered what was wrong, because the people were giving power to leaders who were not helping the country. He did not know whether it was ignorance or whatever that made Ghanaians vote for wrong leaders.

People's Man wondered what was wrong with Ghanaian leaders. He had thought about many things for so long and it all ended up jamming his brain. So what was the best way forward?

People's Man believes Ghanaians must begin to look beyond those political parties who have usurped their democracy. Ghanaians must be wide eyed and wised up. Ever since he was a child, till the time he had grown up, all he had seen was just two political parties taking the mantle of power in turns in the country. When one goes, the other comes. Now the theory is that Ghanaians were making members of these political parties and their families rich. All in his life, he had seen the same faces. So it meant that when one group comes and steals the money they will go and the other group will also come. And by the time the second group got their stomachs full, the first group might have finished their stolen monies and they will force their way back into power. The second group will also go and finish their money and the cycle continued.

People's Man believes Ghanaians must have a plan. And the plan is that they should not allow politicians to tell the people to choose them but rather the people must 'choose' those who rule the country. If Ghanaians really believed power belong to them and that they can give it to whoever they want, then they should forget about these two groups of people who have enriched themselves over the years from the national coffers and give power to a different group based on integrity and competence. This should happen at random, so that, that cycle of the same people enjoying our wealth for ages would break. Only two political parties should not and must not be allowed to keep a country in financial captivity. And they were the ones who were enjoying all the time. Even if they were in opposition, they always have the hope they would come back one day into power and continue the pillage. Full stop, it's all ending this year. A new political party, a fresh political party is coming into power. OPP - Other People's Party- is here. Kofi Bonzi, the shipping and oil magnate is coming. He's the man who is going to break the cycle and give Ghanaians freedom. The future will be bright. There will be jobs, food, prosperity.

He got up and approached the counter.

"Oga APC."

Oga Molu who was sitting comfortably in his chair began the whining again as he got up to serve him. "If you will take your drink you wait for me to sit before you come…."

People's Man ignored him, took the glassful of Akpeteshie and gulped it down. He made the face, placed the glass down and returned to his seat. He wrapped the second marijuana and started to smoke. As the minutes wore on, more people began to troop into the bar mainly from the cinema room. The movies were closed. People's Man knew it was time to go. Now the station was filling up with people.

2

"Anuanom ne adofo me ma mo adwo oo...."People's Man with his megaphone greeted the people. He was dressed in an OPP T-shirt and an OPP cap with OPP bangles on his wrist. The handkerchief in his hand was designed with OPP colors. Ironically, with the weather so cool and the breeze blowing, People's Man was sweating profusely. These are some of the things Akpeteshie can do. The people who he was addressing looked seemingly tired and worn out. Having worked all day, some in the hot day sun, they now had to queue up for 'trotro'– some of which would drive them for hours, going through irritating traffic jams before taking them to their destinations. That was the life in the city of Accra. Right from bed, one needs to go through a lot of frustrations before finally retiring to bed, most of the time very late in the night. Yet ignoring their plight and the long frustrating drive ahead, most in the queue were with him, listening to his message. Maybe it was the only way to forget their worries and frustrations temporarily.

"...many years now since Ghana have had democratic governance. From the beginning, we all thought democracy was the best for us as a people and a country to move forward. Yet you and I know our democracy has not brought us the change we all desired. The two political parties in this country NDC and NPP have not helped this country. We have seen NDC rule and we also have seen NPP rule yet we have gone nowhere. So why should we vote these parties into power again? It is about time we as a people changed our minds. Democracy means power belongs to the people and we give that power to the political parties to rule us. Now if these parties NPP and NDC have not helped us all these years and we continue to suffer, why should we still continue to give them our votes?

"Our country, Ghana, has been blessed by the Almighty with much wealth; I don't know what we don't have in Ghana, gold, diamond, bauxite, manganese, forest, cocoa, land, sea, sun, rain and oil. Other countries have got only one of these or not at all, yet with sensible leadership they are well off and their citizens are enjoying life. We even travel to these nations to enjoy so called 'greener pastures'. So we should ask ourselves why we are where we are. No jobs, no food, no housing, high cost of living, poor health care, bad roads and what have you, all in a country where nature has been so kind to us. This is all because of bad leadership and bad management, corruption and incompetence. And if it's bad leadership and incompetence, then it's NPP and NDC. These two political parties have failed us for they are the only two parties who have ruled this country since our fourth republic democracy began. Now the question I am asking is, are these people the only ones we have in this country or are they the only people who deserve to enjoy the country's wealth? They don't know anything. They cannot help us and we should ignore them. As a people with our destiny in our own hands, we should not sit back for a small group of people to destroy our lives and the lives of our children. Now the youth have no hope, they have no future. I was twenty years by the last elections. Now I am twenty four. I am growing but ask yourselves what kind of adult am I growing into? I have no job, no money and no place to lay my head. Such is the plight of millions of Ghanaian youths whose future looks so bleak. And the more bleak our future, the more bleak the future of this nation. As for me, my advice to everyone is that we should find someone else to lead us. We need committed and intelligent people to lead this country into a brighter future.

"If other countries have been able to do it why can't we? If Malaysia, South Korea, South Africa, Rwanda and many more who don't even have half of what we have got had been able to change their standards of living through good leadership, why can't we? This year's elections must be different. We should give our votes to a different party and ignore NPP and NDC because they cannot take us anywhere. We should vote Kofi Bonzi the billionaire to help change this nation for us. This is a man who will not steal our money but give us the best of leadership. This is a man who through hard work and prudent management changed his life and I believe he can do the same thing for this country. Kofi Bonzi is the man for Ghana and OPP is the party for the future. Vote OPP for jobs and a better life, a better Ghana is what we need.

"Today, everyone is crying, rich and poor alike, even those working cannot find their feet. Salaries are low, cost of living is high. There are high electricity tariffs, high water tariffs, fuel price is rising every day, people cannot afford health care, people cannot afford three square meals, cost of education continues to rise, savings keep going down and our banks are collapsing, businesses are shrinking and Ghana is collapsing. The country currently needs a lifeline and that lifeline is Kofi Bonzi and OPP…."

Now People's Man was fully soaked with sweat and droplets were cascading across his forehead like a waterfall. He had stopped wiping off his face because his OPP handkerchief was sodden and could not absorb anymore. He was now powering up and the sweat poured like rain. "…NPP and NDC are both the same and they cannot help us. All their skills have been exhausted, ideas and all. There is nothing more NPP and NDC could do for our dear nation. I repeat, NPP and NDC are the same, no difference. If NPP accuses NDC of corruption, know that NPP too is corrupt; if NDC accuses NPP of incompetence know that NDC too is incompetent…."
"People's Man bɔ hɔ biom," someone shouted from the queue on his right hand and on the left came "…more fire, more fire…."

"…they are like twins and they've only split up to deceive Ghanaians," People's Man continued. "All they are after is the country's money. Now Ghana is a walking debt. A country of immense resources and all we could do is to borrow to run our economy. What kind of small brain is that? This is the highest form of incompetence I have ever seen in my life. We have everything; all that is needed is a big brain who can think us out of our current bad situation, someone who is not afraid to take bold initiatives.

"Because they want the money to steal, all that NPP and NDC could think of is let's borrow, let's borrow, so money would come quick and they would steal and go away. They are killing us, they are selling the country. One day we will be sitting in this country and someone would come and tell you and me to pack our things and find somewhere to go because our country has been sold to him. Let us be careful because Ghana is all we have.

"Let us vote wisely in these coming elections for your vote is your power. Vote Kofi…."

3

The 'Pentagon' opened around 04:00 every morning but to-day the 'Pentagon' opened late at 05:30am. As Oga Molu opened the wooden gates, you could still see sleep hanging on his face. The late night porn movie had closed very late and that had affected early operation. He had named his little establishment 'The Pentagon' because he believed here was where all the 'action' took place and that his bar was the centre of 'operations'. Initially, the whole place was a bar and a smoking joint. But as more people used to sit around idle after drinking and smoking, Oga Molu decided to operate a video center to make extra money. So he divided the place into two and used half for that purpose. It became successful. African movies were shown during the day from eleven o'clock in the morning to five in the evening. Then, there would be a break after which the cinema would show foreign action movies. From 11:00pm till 00:30am was time for pornographic movies which also attracted a different fee usually much higher yet people patronized. Then the young boys and girls would be seen afterwards hanging behind the kiosks that scattered the place.

'Pentagon' was sitting on a land belonging to Ghana Railway Company and the rail tracks ran in front of the bar. At first the Accra-Nsawam train used to pass occasionally but had now ceased altogether as rail travel took a final dip towards collapse. Now the tracks were used as sleeping grounds for the many hustlers who had travelled down to Accra to find 'greener pastures'.

Behind the 'Pentagon' were rolls of beds covered with mosquito nets which were sold to those who could afford for the night. During the day, these were removed and the space used as parking lot for cargo cars. From the 'Pentagon', running all the way to the main high way that became the Kwame Nkrumah interchange were a line of different businesses ranging from petty trading to heavy duty machine spare parts dealers and 'chop' bars. Another line ran on the opposite side towards Aveno. In front was the railway tracks beyond which were the road that fed the Neoplan station from Kumasi.

After the road stood public toilets and bathrooms with few merchandise stores here and there. Behind these stores and buildings was the Odawna River which Wango Pingo called 'the disgrace of the city' with its stinking black water. Marijuana ghettos and kiosks belonging to squatters ran along the banks of this river ending up with the cattle dealers on the Aveno site.

Oga Molu dealt in all alcoholic beverages available on the market. The only items he never sold were cocaine and cigarette which he deemed as deadly and destructive. Oga Molu believed his bar was the centre of operations because he sold the best Akpeteshie in the whole Circle area and his marijuana was of high grade. The moment the gates were thrown open, four people were alert at the entrance waiting to break their fast. They entered immediately following Oga to the counter.

"Eii Oga, today 'deε' you starve us oo," one of the guys called Fire Service said.

"Please let me sleep a little for me too I am a person," Oga replied.

Most people patronized Oga's Akpeteshie in the morning for best results.

"εyε a susu da, wonim sεεha yaa na yε didi."

"Ye-es," Oga demanded from behind the counter.

All of them bought Akpeteshie. They poured the drink into themselves and within seconds anyone who entered the bar might think these guys had been bereaved. All of them had tears gathered in their eyes. Fire Service rushed out and spat heavily, and then he came back and sat down locking his hands in-between his thighs. One of the three in front of the counter requested a roll of marijuana.

"No please, nobody is smoking now. I need to clean the place. Rocky wake up!"Oga shouted while at the same time hitting the plywood partition of the cinema. Rocky was the young boy who operated the cinema but he doubled up as a helping hand in the morning.

Within fifteen minutes, the whole place was cleaned, glasses washed and benches neatly arranged. 'Pentagon' formally opened for business. And the first person to enter after the clean up was Wango Pingo who many called Doctor. Doctor was a grown up man in his late fifties, a contemporary of Oga Molu. He was the head of an N.G.O engaged in the empowerment and welfare of widows or something. You do not know exactly what they do but he had an office somewhere in Tudu and he was a well-to-do man. Wango's time at the 'Pentagon' was normally in the evenings but when he turned up early like this morning, then you know Wango was in for a long stay. He always enjoyed special treatment at the 'Pentagon' for his bills were always high by the time he was leaving and he paid in full. His favorite drink was Guinness stout. Oga ordered Rocky and one of the three special plastic chairs was produced for Wango. He sat down and ordered for a bottle of Guinness and a roll of Marijuana. Wango took a swig of his Guinness and concentrated on wrapping his weed.

One young man holding a burning cigarette popped up at the entrance.

"Hey Soobolo, take that cigarette away from there," Oga ordered "I have warned you several times; next time I will slap you."

The guy backed off immediately.

"He needs it after taking the cocaine," Wango said.

"I hate those boys," Oga uttered angrily.

"Not you alone. That cocaine is responsible for most social violence and the armed robberies we are experiencing these days," Wango said. "I don't understand why Ghanaian authorities are watching for this thing to take root in this land.

Harsh punitive measures should have been enacted long time to check these hard drugs. Don't you see Thailand and Bangkok? Yes, because drugs bring destruction, even this dollar thing and the struggle to stabilize it, cocaine influences it a lot. For if you consider the amount of cocaine consumed in a day and the fact that it is always available, you will know that it has a lot of pressure on the dollar for you need more dollars to import cocaine. This they will not check but attribute it to all kinds of theories."

"It is their business. Why would they talk about it?" Oga replied. "All this extravagance in politics, where do you think they get the money from?" he asked. "So they will not talk about it. They don't care as long as they make the money. See how the youths are getting spoilt by this cocaine. Some are even dying. That 'rock' and 'tire' are very dangerous."

People's Man entered the bar.

"Eii People's Man," Wango Pingo bellowed, "I heard about you yesterday at Teshie. You are doing a good job. I love guys like you. You've got vision for your country."

"He's bent on bringing NPP and NDC down," Oga said.

"Oga, it's not me alone. It is us all," People's Man replied. "We all together are bringing them down. Ghana is for us and not for them. We should not sit down and watch them destroy this country. When they steal the country's money, they don't even spend it here. They take it outside and their children school outside. But you and I have nowhere to go. Ghana is all we have and we must protect what we have else these people will lick everything and crack the bones. We are all voting against NPP and NDC, you and me. Together, we will succeed in driving them out. One day, they will be bygone words like CPP."

"But CPP is there?" Oga asked.

"It is dead," replied People's Man. "That is how NPP and NDC would become, the living dead."

All of them laughed out loud.

A guy entered and shook the hand of People's Man "More fire People's Man," he said, and then approached the counter and Oga served him.

People's Man got closer to the counter. Now the conversation between Oga Molu and him became subdued as they discussed business. Oga Molu calculated the debt he owed and People's Man paid everything. He then ordered Akpeteshie one Ghana cedi and one roll of weed.

Taking the bench very close to Wango, People's Man sat down and began to wrap his weed.

"Doctor Wango, we are going to vote out this government and Kofi Bonzi would come," People's Man said as he lighted his roll of marijuana.

"It could be possible," Wango agreed, "this man is fast gaining grounds. Very reliable sources tell me he can win this year's elections."

"He has won already Doctor," People's Man uttered confidently.

"You know these NPP and NDC people have been deceiving their followers for too long and now the people are becoming disillusioned," Wango divulged. "They tell them sweet things and big promises when it's getting to elections but afterwards they ignore them. It has happened for too long and now their eyes are opened."

"Deɛ wo mo adi no womo endi nko', we are going to protect the rest," People's Man said.

"That is why I say all the time that none of these contemporary politicians can compare themselves to Nkrumah. Kwame Nkrumah built factories right from Tema to the North. Most of what he did are still serving the nation today. Last time I heard they wanted to resuscitate one of his factories at Komenda or somewhere and it has taken two governments to do this yet they cannot get sugar to flow out," Wango Pingo narrated.

"Two governments?" People's Man curiously asked.

"Yes, two governments, the NDC and the NPP, just one factory of Nkrumah," Wango lamented. "You know Kwame Nkrumah after staying for a long time in America and Europe realized that Africa could easily take over the world's economy. He got to know that all that the west had got was their factories but most of the raw materials feeding those factories were coming from Africa. So the simple theory was, if we could build our own factories for our raw materials, we shall break the flow and Africa would become the centre of trade worldwide. And he started it, right here in Ghana. He was doing it, I saw it with my own eyes, and no one told me. There were agro based industries; we had tomato factories, sugar factories, meat and milk factories, aluminum factory, glass factory, tire factory, a vibrant textile industry, ceramics factory, pharmaceutical companies and more.

"He was also planning factories for our manganese, bauxite and a refinery for our gold. That was Kwame Nkrumah for you. And that was in the 1960s, a time we called 'gyimi mre'. And the marvelous thing was he did all those in a spate of seven years. Just seven years of Nkrumah's rule and Ghana was vibrant with jobs, money, food and good education. The future looked brighter. Now over fifty years after Nkrumah when people say they are modern and more intelligent, what do we see? Instead of adding up to what he started, we have watched what even existed to deteriorate and now they are extinct. Over fifty years and the man Nkrumah has got no size. When the west saw that Kwame Nkrumah's vision was going to bring their economy down, they moved in to overthrow him with the help of our own selfish, greedy, foolish people. Now look at countries like South Korea, Malaysia and the rest who were our contemporaries. They are far advanced. They had moved from Agro-based industries to high tech industries producing mobile phones, computers, cars and heavy machinery while we cannot even find our own Agro- based industries." Wango Pingo lighted his weed whose fire had quenched due to the long talking and drank some of his Guinness which was standing by his chair.

He took a long pull on his roll of weed and continued, "When we were being tormented under military rule and we were fighting for democracy we thought these politicians were going to do something better for this country. So so 'brofo akese', and the GDP and the GOP and the balance of payments and two digit inflation and the, and the, nothing. They don't know anything. Instead of fixing the problem, they have resorted to borrowing and when they borrow they don't use the money for anything better. Small girls and big cars that's all they know, spending Ghana's money aimlessly. Money for nation building ends up on luxury. Now there is oil and still Ghana is the same, Nkrumah's Ghana still better than now. It looks as if there is no competent person in this country except him."

"Me, the people I hate are our professors," Oga Molu chirped in, "when you go to the western world all their inventions and innovations came from and are still coming from their universities. Now our university campuses have become a centre for fashion and social media interactions. They don't know anything. A Ghanaian professor with his mouth can make a supersonic jet and make it fly to America and back in six hours but practically they cannot do anything. It is K.N.U.S.T that I have heard has been making traffic lights. That is all. Traffic lights. When you go to China children make mobile phones. The moment they finish school they are thinking politics because that is where easy money would come from. Ghana's money…."
"They are even into politics before they finish school," Wango Pingo corrected.

More customers trooped into the 'Pentagon'. Some took their drink and left, others also stayed to smoke and gradually the benches were filling up. Belo the Rasta man, his dreadlocks like timber logs also came in. He took two rolls of weed and sat beside People's Man.

"Doctor, long time"

"Belo am alive. I travelled a bit to South Africa but now am back".

"So Doctor, do you think Nkrumah could have succeeded?" People's Man asked after a moment of silence.

"I believe so," Wango uttered. "Do you know why?" he asked.

"No," People's Man replied.

"Ok, of all the continents in the world, it is Africa that is having the most natural resources," Wango divulged. "Africa almost have about seventy percent of the world's natural resources and we only have to add a little brain, some amount of intelligence like Nkrumah was doing and we could be heading for super power. But now…."

"Ah Africans are not smart and we sit back to suffer like this?" People's Man lamented. "Africans are foolish."

"The African is not foolish," Belo retorted. "It's the West making our lives difficult."

"I think People's Man is right. Africans are foolish," Wango agreed.

"Ah Doctor Wango we are not," Belo would not take it. "When Nkrumah was taking us somewhere the West came and overthrew him. It is the West…."

"The CIA overthrew Nkrumah with the help of our own soldiers and that's another evidence of foolishness," Wango asserted.

Belo tried to speak but Wango raised his hand.

"Wait Belo…."

Belo waited.

Wango continued, "Let me tell you a story of one African country. The name was Zaire and their President's name was Mobutu Sese Seko. Zaire is so much endowed with natural resources that even the total value of its resources could be more than the resources of the whole United States put together. They even have uranium, the material used for nuclear energy. And their President Mobutu Sese Seko was the richest man in the land. He was richer than his country. He had about twenty- eight billion dollars in western banks while Zaire was impoverished. Poor inhabitants, bad economy, poor roads, lack of good drinking water, inadequate health facilities and what have you were rife in the country.

"In fact, Zaire was in shambles. With twenty-eight billion dollars sitting in their economy, what did you think the west would do? Watch the money? No, they were using the money to develop their world while even drinking water was not available in Zaire. And ask me where this man got his money from? He got the money by selling the country's resources. After about twenty-seven years of his ruling, his people got fed up with him and overthrew him. He died in a foreign land leaving his twenty-eight billion dollars in the west and it is with them while Zaire continues to suffer. Zaire is now today's Dr Congo. If the African is not foolish, how could this happen?"

"The same thing is happening with our ministers and our presidents," Oga chirped in.

"It is across the whole of Africa," Wango bellowed. "We go and borrow money from the West for the country's development. Our ministers and presidents steal these monies and take them back to the west while the countries pay interest. They have their money back but we are paying interest on the stolen money, and that is the folly of the African politician.

"The same thing goes for Zimbabwe. Formerly, it had one of the best economies in Africa. Then the indigenous people woke up one day and realized that all their lands had been taken away by white farmers. So they decided to take them back. There was a revolt and blacks took back their lands. After taking back their lands, what were they supposed to do?"

"Do what the whites were doing with the land," People's Man answered.

"Good, now go to Zimbabwe," Wango said. "They cannot even feed themselves. The country keeps on going down and down. Recently, I heard Nigeria is fighting to get back money Sani Abacha stole and deposited in the United States."

"Kwame Nkrumah was wrong when he said the black man was capable of managing his own affairs," Oga cut in again.

"He was not wrong, we are," Belo still was not convinced. "It's the whites making things difficult...."

"Belo, if you think like that every day, you cannot rise," Wango Pingo advised. "Everyone is fighting for their own interest and the west is not an exception. Let me tell you about one country called Great Britain. I hope you know it?"

"Yes," Belo admitted.

"Ok you can call it England or the UK whatever," Wango said. "But what I am emphasizing here is, this is a country that has colonized almost half of the countries in the world. Then the time came that these countries fought for their independence and got it. Now with hard work and prudent management, some of these countries are fully independent and are managing their own affairs. Can Britain today tell America what to do?" he asked.

"No," People's Man intoned.

"Can Britain now tell India, Australia or China what to do?"

"No."

"And let me ask you, do you think America wants to see China rise to super power?" Wango queried.

"No," many in the room following Wango chorused.

"Good. Do you think America wants Russia to rise? Or Russia wants America to be the super power of the world? Definitely no. But China is rising whether America likes it or not. America is the super power whether Russia likes it or not. There are attempts to sabotage every day but with determination and wisdom, each is maintaining its stand. So in the same way, if Africans are determined to do something for themselves, nobody can stop them. Sixty something years after independence, Britain still dictates to Ghana. When your ministers or Presidents get the opportunity to travel to the UK, they look so happy as if they were going to heaven. Your minister and your president who were supposed to instill confidence in your country so you could be proud of your country are worshipping another country. That is where they take the money to when they steal it and that is where their children go to school. They forget that ministers and Presidents like themselves made the West what it is today. Now you tell me Belo that the African is not foolish?" Wango demanded.

"Wango it all started with the slave trade and the stealing of our gold, diamond and timber, everything…" Belo struggled to put something together.
"Belo, the Chinese have been slaves before," Wango divulged. "Indians, even Israelites. Can Egypt now compare itself to Israel?
"How did it happen? Careful planning and execution," Wango explained. "Africa only needs knowhow to develop. Knowledge is what is left for us to move forward and as much as this knowledge is readily available, we are not prepared to use it. Ghanaians and most African nations do not even have a national plan which they are following towards development. This government comes and hover around doing what they can do so that money will come into their pockets and walk away. Another comes, ignores what the other was doing and implements their own plans, make money and walk away.

That is what your NPP and NDC have been doing all these years. Nothing better, watermelon heads that is all."

The half-filled bar of youths listening to Wango became down hearted with Wango's narratives. Sadness was written on their faces.

"Africa, what a pity."

"I will not give my vote to any politician anymore, they are all a failure," another said.

"So when are we going to see the light?" one boy asked.

4

The Jubilee Park was filled to the brim. Formerly called Jackson Park, this was where all major political and social events took place in the city of Kumasi. Yellow and green banners were everywhere. Almost everyone present was dressed in OPP colors, a yellow and green T-shirt with Kofi Bonzi's picture boldly imprinted on it. Some matched up with caps and the ladies had muffler and wrappers. Sellers were having a field day. Anything OPP and Kofi Bonzi easily sold out. In the background was the official music of the party, OPP from Naughty By Nature and the crowd joined in the song as they danced to the tune *"...we are the OPP, yeah you know me, we are the OPP everybody say yeah...."*

Somewhere in the middle of the dense crowd, a Soloku dance troop was on display and a big buttocked woman and a man entertained the crowd with their Soloku dance. Pushing out her buttocks, the lady shook the flesh and her buttocks bounced like two footballs being juggled. Meanwhile, the man stuck to her like glue and nothing could separate them as he enjoyed the bouncing flesh wholly pushed out for him. In rhythm to the music, the man would twist his waist from time to time to meet the shaking flesh. The crowd went crazy with applause. Everything was going on.

Kofi Bonzi has brought his campaign tour to Ashanti land and the reception was very great. As was the norm, he had gone to greet the custodian of Ashanti land, the mighty king Otumfuo and his elders and as an open hearted father who welcomed everyone, Otumfuo had not denied him his blessings.

By the time Kofi Bonzi took the stage to address the crowd at the rally, it was almost 3pm. The moment he mounted the stage, all music died down, then shouts and hooting of horns from the crowd took over. Some held up their placards. Some of the placards read "Tired with NPP and NDC", "Kofi Bonzi Ghana's next President", "We are driving the elephant and the umbrella away", "We are hungry, Kofi feed us".

Kofi Bonzi waited for some seconds while he absorbed the frenzy atmosphere and then raised his hand. The whole place became silent.

"OPP!" he shouted and the crowd responded "yeah you know me"

"OPP!"

"Yeah you know me," the crowd chanted again.

"Yes, I think Ghanaians know me. I am Kofi Bonzi and I have come to save our land from the hands of evil greedy men who are collapsing this country. And today the journey through the land to tell my story has brought me to you the people of Kumasi. I will say Kumasi is my home and it was Kumasi that shaped my life. I am right when I tell you I am an Oseikrom boy...."

The crowd gave shouts and applause.

"My father, a civil servant, brought me to this city when I was four. The whole family was in Kumasi for nine years. This was

where I had my basic education and since in life the foundation matters more than anything; I will say the life in me is a Kumasi life. I was thirteen when I left this city but throughout my life I have never forgotten this land. It's a part of me wherever I go.
My brothers and sisters, I know you all shall bear with me that Ghana now is torn into pieces. If Ghana were to be a woman, we will say all her clothes have become rags. She can no longer dress and her beauty is fading away.

"It is not today that this started. All our leaders after Kwame Nkrumah have failed us and we should blame them for the hardship our dear nation is going through. Ghanaians have suffered for too long and it's about time your sufferings got to an end. I, Kofi Bonzi, am here to bring you the relief you are waiting for.
"I was eighteen years old when my father died. I had finished high school at that time and as a young lad from a poor home I could see no light in a country that offered no opportunities. As a young man with ambitions, I realized that none of my dreams could be realized in this country—no jobs, no money, no future.
A country where youths have got nothing to do, they sit idle twenty – four- seven and idleness gradually pushes these youths into the ghettos where they engage in drugs and other nocent activities. I became one of them. In Takoradi, where my family finally settled, I became a ghetto boy hanging in the ghettos along the beaches. Then I had the opportunity to enter a ship one day and I decided not to get out again. I had to hide

in the ship for almost two months and finally I found myself in America.

"Immediately I stepped in America, I found a sea of opportunities, jobs, food, and a future. I worked and with money coming my way, I embarked on education. Eventually, I graduated as a marine engineer and today I am a successful business man with a fleet of ships and an oil field in Papua New Guinea. Presently, my company is mining crude oil off the shores of Ghana and I must tell you we have a lot of oil.

"This country is rich, very rich but those who have ruled this land had not helped the people. They are incompetent, greedy, selfish and I will say evil. I say they are evil in the sense that though they know all your problems they just don't care. All they care about are themselves and their pockets.

"Because if they care, they can do something about your situation for money is there to solve this country's problems. On the other hand, if they say they care and still cannot solve this country's problems, then they are not fit to rule because they don't have the wisdom to.

"Turn around and see. There are riches all around us, I am even sure that even where we are standing now there is gold in the ground. A people that walk on gold and we are hungry. When I was in America, I realized that careful planning and implementation of good policies can lift a country from hardship. All those western countries you see looking beautiful and successful have been like our country before.

"They too have seen some level of hardship in the past but good leadership, commitment and loyalty were the values these countries employed to lift themselves up to the level you see them today. Now everyone longs to be in Europe; everyone longs to be in America. Even your leaders are buying mansions there and they are running away. I am telling you we can make Ghana like America...."

Applause and shouts. The crowd cheered.

"You are president already," someone shouted.

"Yes we have all it takes to turn this country's destiny around for good," Kofi Bonzi continued. "The only ingredients lacking here are wisdom and commitment. When I become President, I will make sure Ghana benefits from all the natural resources God has given the country. Your current leaders are selling this country away, our own gold, Ghana's gold one of the best in the world is being mined by foreign companies and the country is not getting even twenty percent. This goes for all our natural resources including oil. This is unfair. When I become President I will make sure Ghana gets the maximum benefit from our natural resources. Gold would be refined here before export.

"I am going to build technical schools and these shall produce the required artisans with better knowhow to help us take control over our economy which has become so much import based. Those who import raw materials for production in the country shall enjoy very low import duties to boost the growth of local industries. OPP!"

"Yeah you know me!" the crowd chorused.

"My government would make money available for research and researches would be implemented and not left on the shelves. Health insurance would be reliable and better health facilities would be provided. Ghanaians need better health care, OPP!"
"Yeah you know me," the park vibrated.
"When I see a Ghanaian who is hungry, then I get sick. We have good lands, we have rain and we have the sun all year round. Why should my people go hungry? OPP!"
"Yeah you know me."

"I am going to employ the best farming methods to get our land to produce in abundance. I will bring in combine harvesters, tractors and every farming equipment available to help churn out food. I shall build silos and every extra grain or farm product will be preserved. I don't see why Ghanaians should not export food. NPP and NDC leaders are wicked. If you believe it say yeah. OPP!"
"Yeah you know me," the crowd shouted.

"They watch the Ghanaian farmer weed with crude tools. As a result, the Ghanaian farmer gets weak before they get old. NPP and NDC leaders would not think of how to modernize farming to achieve maximum results. They are only interested in your money. I am coming to change this country. OPP!"
"Yeah you know me."

"As a country we must be able to take control of our environment. Things don't just happen. A little effort is needed in doing everything. Our environment must be clean as a people. My government will focus great attention on waste management. We talk cleanliness every day but I don't see even one dustbin in town. Where do you expect people to throw away rubbish? NPP and NDC are always talking about making our cities clean but every day filth is swallowing us. My government will provide dustbins everywhere and the education on hygienic living would be intensified. If you talk about clean environment without dustbins everywhere, I don't know how this could be achieved. This is simple wisdom and NPP and NDC leaders have failed to acknowledge it. Many sicknesses come due to unclean environments. This should not happen. OPP!"

"Yeah…."

Early Monday morning, radio stations across the country were busy discussing Kofi Bonzi's great rally in Kumasi. Though many rallies had gone on during the weekend across the country, every radio station was discussing OPP because of their crowd which was unprecedented and the messages which were powerful and seemed to resuscitate hope for a people who had long waited for someone who could solve their mounting problems. The most popular talk show broadcasted by Peace FM also discussed Kofi Bonzi even though the panelists on the show included representatives from the NPP and NDC. The host who was popularly known as the General focused more on OPP's Kumasi rally.

"...so how did you get that crowd as a totally new political party vying for power?" he asked the OPP representative. "Some are saying you bused people from the villages to achieve this."

"Hahaha," the OPP representative laughed aloud and said "General, did you see any bus at our rally grounds? No, those were people, Ghanaians, fed up with bad governance and were looking for a savior whom they have found in Kofi Bonzi. These people walked on their own to the rally grounds just to listen to the good and assuring messages OPP brings everywhere we go. That crowd was real and not fake. Ghanaians have embraced Kofi Bonzi and he is going to be the next president of this country, a president with a difference."

"Phillip, you heard Kwarteng. He said the crowd was there on their own. No one brought them. Is NDC not afraid when you see something like this?" the host turned to the NDC representative.

"Oh General, this is politics and if you watch crowds you will be deceived. Our brothers in the NPP had a similar crowd before the last elections that brought NDC into power. So crowd alone does not determine the outcome of elections. Those were people who were just curious to see the much talked about Kofi Bonzi who is talking like governance is a child's play. I am rather worried about what the NPP candidate said at their Somanya rally…."

"I haven't asked you about NPP. I said OPP, Philip", the General interrupted.

"Yes I know General, but I must correct certain things the NPP candidate said which were not true…."

"We shall come to that, Bona, Kofi Bonzi at Kumasi. Are you shaken by the crowd?" the host asked the NPP representative.

"Those were people who were bused from the central and western regions. OPP is not telling the truth," NPP man started talking "Kumasi is our strong hold and the people of Kumasi only know one party and that party is NPP. You know, with his money, Kofi Bonzi has been busing crowds to every one of his rallies, but as for Kofi Bonzi, he is not our problem. I am worried about the bad governance NDC is giving Ghanaians. They are just wasting our time. There is nothing going on, no jobs, corruption everywhere, hardship, hardship on the peo…."

"Eii NDC and NPP. I asked about Kofi Bonzi and NDC says NPP and NPP says NDC," the host laughed. "We are talking about OPP. Kofi Bonzi said he would make Ghana like America. Why have NPP and NDC who have ruled the country all these years not been able to do this? Philip, tell me something, you are in power."

"Hmm," Philip sighed before saying, "General, you know our elders say that when you weed with your mouth you don't get hurt. It's easier said than done but I will say that NDC is on the path to making Ghana better. Governance is a process. First things first and the rest follows. You see the massive infrastructure projects NDC is undertaking, we are building roads, interchanges, schools, hospitals and modernizing our airports. All these projects are just the foundations needed for a major take off. These projects and infrastructure are needed if proper development could be achieved and we are on the path to making Ghana a better place. All we ask is for Ghanaians to give us some time, so we can give them a better life…."

"Tweaa, what better life can you give Ghanaians?" Bona interrupted Philip abruptly. "Electricity bills and water bills are rising, health care is becoming expensive every day, corruption is getting out of hand, there is massive borrowing, you people are burying this country in debt…."

"General please this man is wasting my time, it's either you will give me more time or you tell him to shut up. He shall have his time."

"Please Bona let Philip speak," the host came in.

"He's deceiving Ghanaians. NDC cannot do anything for this country. Ghanaians should vote them out...." Bona reiterated.

Philip forced his way back on track and got Bona to keep quiet. "Ghanaians can compare, the records are there and all would testify to the fact that NDC always gives Ghanaians better governance than NPP. We have built more roads, more schools, more hospitals, and more infrastructures. We give Ghanaians good living...."

"That is what I don't want to hear, General," Bona erupted again. "What good living? You build roads and infrastructure, do we eat roads? Do we eat infrastructure? People are not able to pay school fees, hospital bills are unbearable, drivers cannot buy fuel due to high prices and you talk about good living..."

"That's why OPP is coming," Kwarteng uttered. "Because NPP too have not been able to help Ghanaians. Ghanaians have seen NPP rule and have seen NDC rule and Ghanaians can tell me that they are both the same. No plans, no dream for this country. Just long talk and bragging. When NPP came to power, they did nothing just as NDC too is doing nothing. It is Ghanaians who are suffering every day. I urged the people to reject both of them and vote for OPP and Kofi Bonzi massively to save this country".

"Kofi Bonzi said one thing that touched my heart," the General said. "He said he was going to place dustbins everywhere to make sure our cities are clean. Once I was in town and after drinking water, I watched everywhere to find something to throw the bottle in but there was none. I had to put this empty bottle into my bag. By the time I reached home my bag was a litter bin. This simple thing why have NPP and NDC not done all these years because most littering go on because there is no place to put litter? I was very happy by that statement from Kofi Bonzi".

"NPP will see to that when we come to power," Bona answered sharply. "In fact we are going to create a whole ministry for sanitation and make sure Accra becomes the cleanest city in Africa and not just Accra but the whole Ghana...."

"You were in power and you did not do anything, don't throw dust into people's eyes," OPP man rebuked Bona. "This is our promise to Ghanaians and you cannot steal it."

"Waste management is in fact high on our agenda," NDC man started talking, "hundreds of trucks have been ordered and all these are going to help to make the city...."

"I said dustbins everywhere not trucks," the General intoned. "There are certain simple simple things that could make life easier but you politicians focus on bigger things that do not make any impact. Kofi Bonzi also mentioned technical education...."

"NPP will...."

"You cannot do it," Philip snapped.

"We are going to do it. Dustbins everywhere, enhanced technical education, good health care…." Kwarteng started re-echoing Kofi Bonzi's promises.

6

The volume of the radio was high at the 'Pentagon" and the gathered customers, most of them smoking, had become deeply absorbed in the argument going on at the Peace FM studio.

"Ah this host 'dee' I like him so much. Did you hear what he asked the NDC man?" Oga Molu asked Wango Pingo.

"He is an intelligent journalist asking the right questions all the time," Wango agreed. "I don't see why waste management should become so much a problem for us. Walk the whole of Accra and the various cities across the country and you'll see no litter bins yet they talk about clean cities. When people drink sachet water or make waste while in town, where do they expect them to put the litter? In their pockets? They will definitely throw it on the ground. But if we could stop the litter getting to the ground that will be the first step in controlling waste. There are 'bola' cars that are designed to lift dustbins and empty them. So if there were dustbins all around and people are educated to use them, we need about thirty of these trucks in every city and we are going to have a clean environment.

"I have told you these people have got watermelon heads, nothing better in them. Look at the Odawna River, such a strategic drain and A.M.A cannot maintain this river and make it clean. That stinky black water flowing to the sea is full of sickness. It is epidemic flowing out there. Though you don't see it directly, that dirty river is the cause of many sicknesses and deaths every year. It produces mosquitoes, flies and pollutes the air.

"Now, it's even full of silt and I have seen some parts turning into forests. We sit back as a people and watch this spectacle ran through our capital city. It is a disgrace to us as a nation. When they travel outside, don't they see rivers like the Thames running through other nations' cities? They are travelling every day, seeing good things in other countries but they don't learn anything."

"NPP and NDC I don't even know who is better," one guy called Sego said.

Bempa, wearing an NDC T- shirt sitting on the far bench replied, "Tweaa NDC is better than NPP."

That did not go down well with an NPP sympathizer sitting next to him. "Who told you?" he asked. "Can NDC compare itself with NPP?"

"But we give Ghanaians better governance and the records are there to show," NDC man said.

"What better record do NDC have apart from being corrupt and running this country down?" NPP man argued.

"Look at what this guy is saying, NPP and NDC which of them makes life easier when they are in power?" NDC man looked around for support. "Any time NDC is in power money flows, cost of living is low and life is better, you ask everybody."

"'Wa hwεε'. Don't say what you don't know my brother else everyone will laugh at you. It is NPP who have got the men, scholars who know."

"What do they know?" Sego asked.

"Okay one by one let each prove his case," Wango Pingo got interested and opened the floor for them. NDC man had the big mouth and overpowered his NPP fellow. Wango gestured to the NPP man to wait so they could hear the NDC man first.

"Democracy started with NDC," he began "that time life was good, cost of living was low and Ghana was better. I remember petrol prices were very low, electricity and water tariffs were also low and I could not say Ghana was the best but compared to the time NPP came to power, Ghanaians were cool. Then NPP came and took us to HIPC. Within a year, petrol prices had rocketed. Book-long people with 'brofo akese', they called something deregulation and the and the. Then cost of living began to rise. To add insult to injury, they changed the currency and Ghana became hard.

"I remember before the currency was changed, ice water sold for five pesewas but immediately after the change ice water became ten pesewas and now twenty pesewas. Things that sold cheap suddenly became expensive because people took advantage saying there were no change and the sort. Things that sold for eighty pesewas became one cedi; one cedi became two cedis and so on...."

"This is cheap talk," NPP man rebuked. "Before democracy, NDC previously PNDC had drowned this country into so much debt there was nothing we could do but take advantage of the HIPC initiative which slashed our international debt by almost two thirds. That allowed the then NPP government to get money to run the country. Inflation was so high our currency was nothing but a bunch of papers. More money chased few goods and people had to carry large sums around. And to make things simple, the currency needed to be modified to make transactions simple and easy. That was brilliance. NPP came to build our roads and upgrade our infrastructure which was totally dilapidated. Ghana began to stand on its feet. It was NPP that discovered oil for this nation...."

"Then what happened?" NDC man came in vehemently. "We are talking about cost of living and you are talking about infrastructure. If I am hungry what is road to me?"
"See the mentality," NPP man said. "We should eat our money in our mouth and leave the country to rot? That is NDC for you. They 'chop' the money and leave the country to rot. That is why you see a lot of money in town when NDC is in power. 'Buga buga' they rule the country anyhow without careful planning."
"Even then NDC has built more infrastructure than NPP. If you like let's count....."

"Me, my problem was what NPP used the HIPC money for," Oga lamented from behind his counter. "You go around the country and you will see public toilets with the inscription 'HIPC benefit.' Such an amount of money Ghana benefitted, we could not use this money to do anything better but toilets."

"They could have even built just two factories and these factories could have employed thousands of people directly and indirectly," Wango supported. "Now what have become of those toilet facilities? They are all rotten. And that is the difference between Kwame Nkrumah and our contemporary leaders. Nkrumah's projects survived the times, valuable projects that still exist and are benefitting the country sixty years after. See Tema harbor, Takoradi harbor, and Tema motorway. Tarkwa roads were built just sixteen years ago but go to Tarkwa now and see, the whole town is full of dust.

"Tema motorway is over sixty years and it's still better than the roads these current governments had built. Compare Nkrumah's universities and schools to the ones these NPP and NDC people had built. Everything Nkrumah did was valuable and beneficial to generations but these people do shoddy work and they steal the money."

"That is why we have gone nowhere," People's Man who had sat silently all this while came in. "They don't do anything better even though the money is there. The minister would give millions to his girlfriend and say there is no money for roads. They will buy big cars and throw big parties and say there is no money.

"That is why we all must come together and vote for OPP because we had given NPP the chance and they could not help us and we have given NDC the chance and they too could not help. Every day big promises but they cannot deliver. We cannot afford to waste time on these people anymore. We must change our hands if we want to change Ghana for the better. Kofi Bonzi can do something. If he comes and he also fails, we change him and continue to change until we find the right people. NPP and NDC will take us nowhere."

"Oh People's Man, Kofi Bonzi cannot win power or do anything, you are wasting your time. NDC will deliver, let's maintain them for the next four years or even more years and Ghana will change," NDC man rubbished People's Man's suggestion.

"That is one thing I hate about NDC and their politics," Wango retorted. "They are always saying it cannot be done when someone from another party makes promises. Did you hear that guy on the radio station saying NPP cannot do it? Always portraying pessimism. What I know is when there is a will there will definitely be a way. There is nothing that cannot be done, if there is the will to do it.

"They talk as if their brains have been walled and they cannot think further. Our country is in the hands of people who do not think anything is possible? Very bad. As for me I will say we should vote for people with bigger promises like Kofi Bonzi and hold them accountable. In that way less money is wasted as they struggle to fulfill their promises and Ghana shall benefit in the long run. You people are young and you should not waste time following these politicians. Because when they make their money, they don't help you. I am older than all of you and I am telling you, if good and intelligent people rule, this country would be better off. Other countries were worse than Ghana but they have made it. Don't allow these politicians by their incompetence deceive you that we cannot become advanced. We can if we get the right people to rule like Nkrumah did."

NDC man and NPP man became silent. None talked again. Meanwhile the argument on Peace FM was raging.

"We came with health insurance…." NPP man was speaking.

"But you collapsed it before you were out of power; we came to maintain it…." NDC man bashed.

"How much do you now owe stakeholders?" NPP man asked.

"Both NPP and NDC have failed when it comes to the health of Ghanaians…." OPP man came in.

"So won't you keep quiet for one person to talk?" The host nicknamed the General struggled to keep his panelists in control.

7

During the afternoons when the video show had started at the 'Pentagon', the bar usually became serene and less busy. People's Man got an empty bench at a corner and stretched himself on it. More Akpeteshie, more weed and after eating he felt lazy and sleepy. Today would be a holiday. He was not going to work. Ignoring the occasional shouts from the video room as the movie got more interesting, People's Man was asleep within minutes. He was still on flight when he felt someone shaking him.

He woke up to find out his visitors were his Senior High School friends. These boys being day students had landed straight at the 'Pentagon' after school.

They were occasional visitors and normally they were always there for the weed. These boys along with other students who flaunt the ghetto easily strike friendship with People's Man because of his educational background. Being a senior high school graduate himself, these up-and-coming students usually saw him as their senior and some called him so. Sometimes they discussed school when they were 'high' and had got nothing to do. People's Man would reminisce about his days at school and the youths would also tell him new things on campus. Most times they solved questions and People's Man tried to teach them one or two things ahead of time.

But more to these intimate relationships was the 'connections' these boys bring and being unable to sell these 'connections' they relied on People's Man as their middle man for buyers. People's Man knew a lot of buyers who bought everything regardless of where they were coming from, and though they bought these items at very cheap prices, they were at least reliable and provided a ready market for anything marketable. People's Man got up and sat upright. The two students immediately sat on either side of him sandwiching him between them. One of them dug into his backpack and produced two fresh phones and a new digital camera.

"People's Man, this one fast fast oo I need money. Poppi just returned yesterday from U.S and I bust them, they are fresh".

The sleep vanished from People's Man's eyes immediately he saw the items. Money has come. He took the phones and camera and examined them. The phones were home second hand and the digital camera was brand new.

"So how much do you want for them?" he asked.

"People's Man make wild even five hundred is cool."

People's Man's heart started racing. The camera alone could cost about a thousand Ghana cedis. He took the items, found an empty polythene bag on the ground and placed them inside. Then he told the students to wait for him. As he got up and was leaving the 'Pentagon', he heard them call Oga who all the while was sitting behind the counter which hid his view from what had gone on. Oga got up and People's Man heard him as he was leaving, "I have told you boys not come here with school uniforms...."

"Oga it was an emergency, give us two rolls, Oga, Oga, Oga Molu the international...." he heard them flattering him as he stepped out and crossed the rail tracks.

First, he passed Baah's place, his friend who was a mobile phone repairer and inquired of the Phones' prices. Baah told him the phones were expensive ones and the two could cost about two thousand four hundred cedis. The camera, Baah said, was about thousand five hundred cedis. Guided by this information, People's Man took the items and headed for Adabraka official town area. There he had an Alhaji who was a scraps dealer and also bought marketable items. It was Alhaji Sani who had got the money and taste for good things.

He passed where the call girls were. They were sitting in front of their rooms which were built with woods. As he passed, he heard them calling "...come for short, come for short...."

People's Man ignored them though he could see fresh young girls and those were new faces. He entered the mechanics yard and headed for a heap of scrap metals which was Alhaji Sani's place.

Alhaji Sani was sitting with friends drinking 'Ataya' and he immediately told People's Man to enter the rubber tent which was his makeshift office. He got up and followed him in.

"Eii, my friend long time no see. You have ignored me these days."

"Alhaji ino be so, ibi goods wei ino de come," People's Man explained.

"The boys these days don't get goods. I don't know why," Alhaji Sani expressed concern.

"The system hard oo Alhaji but today I bring you better goods, your taste Alhaji. I know you like good things," People's Man cajoled.

"Eii my friend," Alhaji patted his back, "make I see what you have got."

People's Man emptied his polythene bag and silence ensued as Alhaji took a careful look at the items. He gave a big smile after a while.

"Eii my friend so this how much?" he asked People's Man.

"Alhaji this one ibi some Boga oo wey ibring. They are fresh and he needs someone who can buy them good. I could think of no one but you," People's Man said.

"Yes, yes I have seen they are from home and they are good. He says how much?" Alhaji Sani reiterated.

"Alhaji he says he needs money for some matters"

"And he says how much?" Alhaji Sani kept asking.

"He says all of them two thousand," People's Man finally uttered.

"Eii my friend things are not good these days oo they no dey buy things. Make you reduce am," Alhaji pleaded.

"Alhaji go pay how much?" People's Man asked.

Alhaji Sani stood meditatively for a while "Make I give you seven hundred," he said finally.

"Eii Alhaji the phones be iphones oo original and the camera be brand new even store sef be two thousand," People's Man contended.

"I know my friend but money no dey and you know how we do these things ino be store matter," Alhaji Sani opined.

"I know Alhaji, I know but do something, seven hundred paa de he no go take."

Alhaji Sani who always negotiated to his advantage, told People's Man to sit down. He vanished for a while and came back.

"I went to check the phones," he said. "They say they are good. You let me give you nine hundred, money no dey. You know I was not prepared. Just consider and next time I go make you fine."

They pulled and tossed. Finally People's Man succeeded in pushing Alhaji Sani to add fifty cedis to make nine hundred and fifty.

"Deal," Alhaji said and dug a hand into his Jalabia pocket bringing out a bundle of fifty Ghana cedi notes. He counted nine hundred and fifty and handed the money to People's Man who counted them again to crosscheck.

People's Man shoved the money into his rubber bag and came out of the tent, squinting as the late afternoon sun fell on his face. As he took the bend that led back to the call girls' area a smile beamed on his face. To-day was his lucky day.

"Come for short, come for short...." People's Man did not hear them.

He turned to the next public toilet he found and entered. He paid the woman and took a toilet tissue. But People's Man was not going to toilet; he only wanted a safe place to take his share of the money. He sat on the closet and brought out the money; he counted three hundred cedis out of it and pocketed it somewhere. He then left six hundred and fifty in the polythene bag and came out, this time he headed straight to 'Pentagon'.

When he entered, he found his friends smoking and arguing. One had his shirt removed and was wearing only singlet. The topic on board was Stone Boy and Shatta Wale. One said Stone Boy was gentle and he liked his style but the other said Shatta Wale's songs made him want to fly. Oga was playing 'Dem confuse' on his radio, the volume lowered due to the video show. Only the voices of these students could be heard as they deliberated on their favorite stars. The moment they saw People's Man without their items, they shouted "Yoo People's Man, yoo yoo" and they started dancing to the tune of the music on play.

People's Man sat them down and explained everything to them. He gave them the six hundred and fifty cedis. The bare-chested guy took the money and counted them. With his roll of weed in his teeth, he smiled and danced once more. He then counted a hundred cedis and gave it to People's Man. He passed to him the joint they were smoking. He dressed up and they later left, happily.

People's Man turned to Oga who was standing behind the counter watching all that was going on "Oga A.P.C.," he shouted out. "These are the Daddy Bs oo. Their fathers are the ones chopping Ghana's money, I wonder why they even come to the ghetto, all the way from West Airport residential."

"Nkwadaa bɔne," Oga said. "It starts like this, small 'connections' while at school and when they become ministers and public servants, it turns to big 'connections'. They learn the stealing at an early age and graduate with it into the various offices and just like their fathers, they plunder with their pens adding one zero to two zeros and two zeros to three zeros."

"Hmm ɛyɛ asem oo," People's Man muttered.

"Eii People's Man, today you get money oo," Oga said as he poured the drink.

"Oga what I for do, Ibe God oo Oga, Ibe God, you see I was asleep when they came. I didn't have Kobo but God always cares for his children. O Nana Nyame gye nsa," People's Man poured a bit of his Akpeteshie on the ground and threw the rest behind his throat, hitting his chest as the hot alcohol descended into him. He sighed and placed the glass down. Tears were gathering in his eyes as he said "Oga this Akpeteshie be A'one."

"Today there is money, pay me and give me my share," Oga said laughing.

People's Man dug out the fifty cedi notes the boys gave him and gave one to Oga. Oga gave him his change. People's Man again gave Oga ten cedis and said, "Oga, give me one roll and take the change."

"People's Man, People's Man….." Oga sang his name as he handed him the marijuana. People's Man took the weed and found a seat.

After smoking, he got up and decided to leave. At the threshold of the 'Pentagon' gate, he paused and took a look at the tall building ahead of him which was the headquarters of Vodafone Ghana. That was where he was heading to. He was going to Odo Rise restaurant. Today he must 'chop' better.

8

The President had been forced from office. He was on an extensive tour of the country commissioning the numerous projects he had done during his three and a half years rule. There rode among his convoy uncountable journalists, having been paid to highlight every one of the many projects the NDC government had undertaken across the country. He had commissioned many but there were still more to unveil. The political atmosphere was very tense and despite his many achievements, news from the ground was not good. The opposition was getting stronger and stronger everyday despite the government's efforts to show Ghanaians he's been working hard.

Now the new party, OPP, headed by the business tycoon Kofi Bonzi had joined NPP, another strong opposition. The President knew that two strong opposition parties were havoc to his hold on power. Many Ghanaians were refusing to acknowledge the great effort he was putting in to bring the country back on its feet. In spite of the numerous commissioned projects and the intensive media highlights, his opponents were still succeeding in convincing Ghanaians that he was not working. Campaign strategies and plans were failing and the President knew that he must do something. Thinking through, he chose to make unpopular the leaders of the two strong opposition parties by tainting their image.

The tour had presently brought him to the Volta region, a region supposed to be a stronghold of the NDC but the opposition was penetrating strongly. Here, he commissioned about eight schools and a big modernized hospital, after which his convoy headed for the rally grounds.

NDC colors were flung everywhere and as the President got out of his car to mount the stage, Volta women with big backside danced 'Abaja' in front of him guarding him with all 'the good things' to the stage. Others threw their cover cloths on the ground for him to walk over.

 When he mounted the stage, the whole place beamed, and charged with his presence, the crowd gave loud applauses and shouts.

"Ɛyɛ zu!" the President shouted into the loudspeaker.

"Ɛyɛ za," the crowd responded.

"Ɛyɛ zu!"

"Ɛyɛ za!"

"NDC!"

"Idey be keke."

"Ghana is better off with NDC and we would not allow corrupt incompetent people to come into power to take us back," the President started speaking. "Immediately I took power I started putting up programs that are going to help with the fast acceleration of the country's development. There is evidence everywhere, schools, roads, hospitals, markets and these are supposed to be the foundation upon which we would build a better future. I don't think we should allow the NPP or anyone to take us backwards by bringing them into power. Everybody know how NPP made living hard for Ghanaians when they came to rule this country until NDC came in to put this country back on track. The leader of the NPP, everyone knows, is a violent and tribalistic man who is going to divide this country if he is voted into power. These people's records have shown to be corrupt and we cannot leave our country in the hands of corrupt filled men. Ghana is moving forward with NDC, ɛyɛ zu!"

"ɛyɛ za," the crowd chorused.

"I have now heard there is another man coming, but all of you will bear with me that Kofi Bonzi is a fraudulent man and this country is headed for doom if our destiny is thrown into the hands of such a fraudulent person."

The president was referring to a case that took place in the United States where a Ghanaian was arrested by the FBI for fraud and it was reported in a Ghanaian newspaper that it was Kofi Bonzi. Later, evidence showed the fraudster's name to be Kofi Bona and not the popular Kofi Bonzi. The newspaper had retracted the story and offered apologies. Yet still the President in the name of politics was hammering on the story to score points - as usual, politics, offering the freedom to say whatever one desired of his opponents just to paint them black.

"He has been defrauding people across the world and as the international community has got to know him, he's now turning to Ghana thinking Ghanaians do not know who he is. I know Ghanaians to be wise people who would not allow a fraudster to rule this country and collapse the economy which NDC over the last three years has taken the pain to make strong. Ɛyɛ zu!"

"Ɛyɛ za," the crowd went wild.

"If NPP come to power we are going to see violence and division and if the so called OPP is allowed power, Ghana will collapse. So fellow 'akatamansonians' and Ghanaians what is the best we can do? The best we can do is to maintain NDC so that Ghana would see more development, acceleration and freedom. Ɛyɛ zu!"

"Ɛyɛ za," the crowd chanted.

"As I'm talking now, NPP is divided. And if we have someone who cannot unite his own party members, how can this person unite the whole of Ghana if he is voted into power. Kofi Bonzi is already deceiving his party people, promising them things but he is not able to deliver. And if you have a person who cannot fulfill his promise to his party followers, how much more expect him to fulfill his promise to Ghanaians? The only better option left for our dear country is NDC which has shown commitment to the development and improvement of the living standards of Ghanaians. Sometimes I know things are hard but I urge you to take heart we shall get there. The foundation has now been built, you have seen the many developmental projects my government has put on the ground. My second term is going to ensure that Ghanaians get money in their pockets. Better life awaits everyone. Ɛyɛ zu!"

"Ɛyɛ za."

"NDC!" the President shouted into the microphone.

"Ide be keke," the crowd responded gleefully.

9

The 'Pentagon' as usual was beaming with life this morning. Customers trooped in and out and those who chose to smoke sat down and listened meditatively to political comments on Oga's radio – which was tuned high every morning until the video show started – passing their own comments here and there as politicians deliberated on issues concerning the country. This morning, Oga's radio dial found Okay FM and currently on the line was the spokesperson for the NPP evaluating the President's campaign speech at the Volta region.

"...we will not say the President has not worked," he was answering a question from the host who highlighted some of the numerous infrastructures the NDC government was commissioning. "He has built a lot of infrastructure but what the NPP as a party is saying is that, every government after all builds infrastructure. We built Tettey Quarshie interchange and they built Circle interchange. Now cars move faster from Kwame Nkrumah interchange and they go and pile up at Obetsebi-Lamptey circle. When power is handed to us, we will also construct an interchange at Obetsebi-Lamptey circle to ease the flow to Kaneshie. So what I want to say is, for infrastructure, it is for every government to build but what we are putting across is the failure of the NDC government to enact policies to bring relief to the people.

"Now, health insurance is not working, taxes are too high and manufacturers and importers are crying. Electricity bills are accelerating, fuel prices are unbearable, and the 'trotro' and taxi drivers who use fuel everyday cannot feed their families. The NPP believe that government taxes on these amenities are too much and especially, government can reduce its taxes on fuel so that the prices will generally come down. It can do likewise for electricity and water. People cannot pay their rent; neither can parents pay their children's school fees.

"Now this government is on a borrowing spree and the debt of the country is tumbling over. The country now is turning to I.M.F to get the economy running. This government borrows money to construct infrastructure and the President says he is running a country. This kind of governance can even be done by a twelve year old. There are no jobs; people cannot pay their bills, no food on the table. This is the most incompetent government in the history of this country and Ghanaians need to vote this government out and bring the NPP.

"When the NPP come to power, we are going to improve education, build factories and get health insurance going. We are going to improve agriculture, fuel prices will be drastically reduced so the taxi and 'trotro' drivers can work and feed their families. Electricity tariffs will come down and we shall give tax relieves. All the roads in the country now are spoilt but this NDC government says it has built roads. When NPP comes, we are going to repair all the bad roads in the country. Ghanaians need better roads to drive on.

"We are going to give one million dollars to every constituency annually to help accelerate development in the various constituencies. That will be bringing development down to the people...."

"You said one million dollars to every constituency? Where are you going to get that money from?" the host asked.
"We are going to take it out of the budget. We will take the money out of next year's budget. So we are starting early next year when we come into power. We are on a fast track to develop the country. There is money in this country but due to bad governance, NDC people don't see this money and Ghanaians are the ones suffering from this sort of incompetency. NPP will come and Ghanaians will be relieved...."

An argument suddenly erupted at the 'Pentagon' that threw the radio voice to the background. The bunch of smokers, a mixture of NDC and NPP supporters, picked up the argument.
"This man is a liar, NPP cannot do anything. All this be 'mouth talk'," one NDC supporter bellowed. "Do they know how to govern a country? They are saying what will bring them into power. They are a bunch of hungry elephants. They will remain in the bush; elephants are not wanted in the city. Ghana cannot feed elephants, they shall 'chop' everything, akronfo."

"Waa hweɛ'. You NDC people argue blindly" an NPP man replied. "You, look into your life and tell me you are okay. Just tell me everything is well with you. See the heat this NDC government is taking us through and you sit down talking nonsense when 'Aban papa' is coming to take us out of our problems. Isn't all that the NPP man saying on the radio true? Tell me they are not true. You yourself you don't know where this life is taking you to. This NDC government cannot do anything and if better people are coming, you sit down there talking off your head".

"Hoo NPP aman muo papa bɛn? Master leave us let us chew our kelewele. NDC ide be keke. ɛyɛ zu, ɛyɛ za all the way," NDC man said adamantly.

"So you people still follow this NPP and NDC?" People's Man who presently had entered the 'Pentagon' asked. "We have had NPP governance and we have had NDC governance yet still none can do anything better and Ghanaians still continue to suffer. So when are we going to learn a lesson and toss these parties aside? I think we all should come together and try someone else. Let's vote Kofi Bonzi and try him also to…."

"Oh People's Man 'ma yen dwen yen ho,' Kofi Bonzi cannot do anything. Where are the people he is going to rule this country with even if he wins power? He does not have the men who could help him rule," NDC man rubbished People's Man's suggestion.

"Kofi Bonzi is a thief," NPP man came in. "Vote NPP for a better Ghana. NPP have got the men, 'akukudam' who will change this country in seconds. Eshi wrado wrado."

"Why did they not change the country and make it better when they came into power?" People's Man inquired.

"But have you forgotten how sweet Ghana was when NPP was in power?" NPP man asked. "Inflation went down, NPP brought health insurance and for the first time pregnant women attended hospital for free. There was abundance of food and money was in the system. Have you forgotten?"

"And then what happened?" People's Man asked.

"Ghanaians made the mistake and gave power to this NDC government who has come to overturn everything and they still insist we let them continue their 'aman muo bɔne'. No, we are fed up; they are going this year...."

"And Kofi Bonzi is coming," People's Man insisted.

"NDC is going nowhere; it is the only hope Ghana has," NDC man said vehemently.

"Tweaa....."

10

Time for elections was fast approaching and at the various political party headquarters, party leaders were busy evaluating strategies that could help them win the elections which had become so competitive and uncertainty hung in the air for everyone. In most previous elections it had been easy predicting outcomes depending on performance, but this year was different. The new face that has emerged was fast gathering momentum and the two main political parties that had been at the forefront of the country's elections were now highly troubled. They were aware of Kofi Bonzi's rising popularity which was highly threatening.

At the NDC headquarters, party leaders were busy discussing how to rig the elections if possible in order to maintain power. Maintaining power was crucial because a loss was going to set a record which would be very bad for the party. Throughout the history of the country's democracy no government has been voted out of power in its first term but this was what was threatening to happen to the NDC government if they did not take care.

The general secretary was presently putting up a suggestion which everyone listened to attentively, nodding their heads intermittently as they all agreed on a point raised here and there.

"…if we don't take care and allow these people to grab power, especially NPP, we will be doomed and disgraced," he said. "Number one, you all will agree with me that they had raised concern over the last elections being rigged and that we did not win but the E.C helped us. If we don't win hands down, this assertion of theirs would gain grounds and that would be a bad record for us. Second, if these people win power especially NPP, they are going to throw aside all the programs we are embarking on to move this country forward and finally, you know how these people play their politics. It will be difficult for us to grab power again if we allow them to win the elections. I think we should do everything in our power to avoid that. We are in power and we should take advantage of our incumbency.

"Whether NPP or OPP we are winning and I have called this meeting to invite ideas as to how we could win this election no matter what happens. Rigging is my first suggestion because it seems as if the people are listening to the lies they are giving them."

"And how do we do that because these people, especially the NPP, who look so aggressive for power are now very vigilant and they are not going to blink an eye for a second," the chairman of the party who felt his position would be compromised if the opposition took power said with urgent tone.

"I think we should use Volta. That is our world bank and we could easily add more ballot papers to put us ahead. Then we shall find ways to add a little little to other constituencies."

"What ways do you suggest?" the general secretary asked the central regional chairman who made the suggestion.

"Let us use Togo. We can prepare the ballot papers there and bring them in," the central regional chairman expounded.

"How?" the national chairman asked.

"Simple. We can buy coffins, stuff them with the thumb printed ballot papers and drive them in, using a hearse like some corpse is being brought. We are in power and we control the borders, so coming in would not be a problem."

"And how do we add these ballot papers to ballot boxes at the polling stations since each party has got representatives around?" the national youth organizer asked.

"Confusion," the central regional chairman opined.

"What do you mean by confusion?" the general secretary inquired.

"Let's get these macho men. We can employ them, find something for them, and they will create confusion at the polling stations. In the midst of this, they would steal the ballot boxes away. Police men who would be bribed would then chase them and by the time they bring back the boxes our papers might have been added. These macho men can also intimidate the other party representatives and put fear in them. A lot could happen to our advantage in the midst of all the commotions you know," the central regional chairman said.

"So how many 'dead bodies' could be brought in?" the national chairman asked.

"Let's make it one coffin to avoid suspicion. We can request for an extra large one and that can take thousands of ballot papers," the greater Accra regional secretary contributed.

"That is for Volta, what about other places especially Ashanti and the eastern corridors where these NPP people have got massive support?" the national chairman asked.

"The same thing will go on," said the central regional chairman. "Confusion and more confusion but this must be done latently and craftily so people would not lose confidence in the elections and call for a re-run."

"Confusion. I think that is a good idea. And where do we get the boys because we need loyal macho men who will not give us away," the general secretary asked.

"Let's check the Zongos. That is our grounds. The Zongo boys would be more appropriate, they understand violence better," the Ashanti regional youth organizer said.

Everyone nodded in the room. It seems 'confusion' was a good idea.

"What about the E.C...." someone started a suggestion.

"No! Elections are won at the polling stations and the E.C has little control when it comes to that. So let's deal with the polling stations," the general secretary said. "I will say the regional secretaries should go and begin immediately to organize the boys who would undertake this course."

"And we need to find money for them you know?" the western regional secretary said.

"That is not a problem," the general secretary assured. "I will consult with chairman and …."

The general secretary of the NPP accepted the hug from his wife immediately he entered into bed. They had not seen themselves for over three weeks as he toured the country busily campaigning. This was a crucial election for him. The outcome of this year's elections was going to determine the future of his political carrier. He had taken the party to two elections but they have lost all. He knew that the party would do a major reshuffle if this year's election was not won. With this pressure on the heads of all the party leaders, intensive campaigning was the norm and that meant sacrificing time with family and wife. It was around one in the morning when he reached home. Throwing his briefcase and laptop somewhere, he had immediately dashed for the bathroom.

Presently in the arms of his wife, he knew the woman was missing him dearly as she continued to hold him tight, planting a kiss on his lips which he parted to accept her tongue. They kissed deeply for a while and he felt his wife's hand finally exploring his body. They were still kissing when he heard his emergency phone ringing. He froze and he knew his sudden pause did not go well with his wife. Yet he got up and grabbed his phone which had finished ringing. He was checking the call log to see who called when the phone started ringing again. The name on the screen was the party's national chairman.

He picked the call.

"Bernard where are you?"

"I am home chairman"

"Organize an immediate meeting. We are meeting at headquarters in one hour. I have just received information that NDC leaders have met to discuss how they are going to rig the elections and they have come up with very funny plans. We cannot afford to waste time to counter them. Please treat this as an urgent issue, see you in one hour"

"Okay chairman"

The general secretary immediately organized a conference call alerting all party leaders to meet at the headquarters in an hour or forget about winning the elections. Response was positive.

He ended the call and turned to his wife who waited longingly on the bed.

"There is an emergency sweet ...."

"Don't talk to me," his wife snapped. "Am fed up, go and marry your politics."

He got closer to explain but she pulled the bed cover over her head and ignored him. The general secretary stood for a while watching his wife with a heavy heart. He understood all her actions. She was lonely and desperate but what can he do? This was what he's got himself into. Politics was now the blood that ran through his veins. If he had known it was going to get him this far, maybe he would not have started it in the first place. His children had not even seen him for over two months. He would come home to meet them asleep and before they woke up, he was gone. Now his wife who evidently needed him was losing him to politics. As he found something to wear, he wondered how he was going to appease the woman and bring her love back on track. Time will tell. He placed a kiss on the cloth that covered her head and proceeded to go out.

"Collins, are you asleep?" He went to his boy's quarters and called his driver.

"Master am here."

"Come out, we are going to the party headquarters."

Politics can bring people with a common goal together easily and it's amazing how this happens. Within the stipulated one hour time, all the top shots in the NPP had met at the party's headquarters and before 2:10 am they were attentively listening to a recorded version of the NDC meeting sent via WhatsApp by a special agent they've planted inside NDC headquarters. Getting information like this was relevant to making decisions about the course ahead.

After listening to the recordings, the leader of the NPP straightened up and said "But we also have got Zongo boys?"

"Sure," the general secretary agreed. "And we must move fast to form a vigilante group to monitor the ballot boxes because we cannot trust the police. We also must get macho men to deal with this."

"So what happens if there should be a clash because our men would be having no weapons while NDC have the security forces on their side and that is a disadvantage" the Accra regional chairman came up. "I suggest we make noise of this recording. Let NDC leaders know we are aware of their plans. In that way we are going to deal with them openly and we shall succeed in forcing them to drop their plan."

"No! You don't know these people; they shall go ahead if they find out that we don't have a backup plan," the general secretary said. "Let us organize our own boys, give them training and deploy them at the various polling stations. If something happens, they shall defend it, if nothing happens, then, fair enough. But I am saying we should be prepared for anything because these people are bent on maintaining power yet they are not doing anything for this country."
"So should we get the boys?" the national youth organizer asked.
"I think so," the chairman of the party gave his consent.
"I also agree with chairman," the general secretary said.
"So what is the plan?" the Accra regional chairman demanded.

"Secretary, get all party executives and regional chairmen in all regions across the country and ask them to gather as many of the macho men in their constituencies as possible," the national chairman commanded. "We shall schedule a meeting to brief them on how to monitor the ballot boxes to prevent the rigging NDC is planning. We need to be vigilant and we need this vigilante group. From what we have listened to so far, it becomes imperative to have one."

"And you heard them talking about money for their boys, how do we cater for our own?" the greater Accra regional chairman asked.

"We shall see if we can make some contributions for them. But most importantly let them understand that if they can help the party come into power, we will give them jobs and money," the leader of the NPP said.

"Ok when day break, I will send messages across to the regions and start following up the next day to monitor proceedings," the general secretary assured.

"It's very important general. Very, very important."

"And the ballot papers from Togo how do we…."

People's Man forgot his shoeshine box when he got money. Every day it was Akpeteshie, weed and Odo Rise restaurant. After seven days he came to himself, that he was in Ghana and that all was not rosy as he thought. He became upset and angry as he found his box and dressed up for work. Four hundred Ghana cedis and he could not spend it for even a month. Just Akpeteshie, the cheapest alcoholic drink on the market, a few rolls of weed and Odo Rise restaurant for one week and the money was gone. In Ghana you get the money big but it was gone in a few days. Yet the government always echoes inflation reduction that it had dropped to a single digit. All these were the big talks just to deceive, like Wango said last time. Big big English and terms but when the reality dawns, you realize nothing has changed. It was the same old life, difficult, hard and this was pushing man to hustle every day. Hustling that brought nothing because money could not do anything better. Just food and a little alcohol and weed and whatever you got was gone and the cycle began again.

He watched the blazing sun with resentment as he placed his hat on his head and stepped out of his little kiosk which served as his room, home and everything. For a week now he had not gone to the station to campaign but the four hundred cedis that was gone in a short time got him mad. He decided to start again to make sure this current government was voted out to make way for Kofi Bonzi who will turn the country around. He was going to bring confidence into the nation that had got everything except good people to run it.

"Shine, shine," he hit his box with a stick to call attention "shine, shine your shoes, shine your shoes," he hit hard on the box.

At the Neoplan station he got his first customer. People's Man gave the man a pair of flip flops to stand on as he took his pair of shoes to brighten up for him.

"Are you travelling?" he asked his customer.

"Yes I'm going to Kumasi. Please be quick, the bus is filling up," the customer replied.

"Don't worry I will finish soon," People's Man assured.

People's Man became aware of a bangle on the man's wrist and the color told him the man belonged to NPP.

"Are you NPP?"

"Yes but what else do you want me to be? Party 'papa paa baako pɛ'. Why are you NPP too?" the man asked People's Man.

"No, OPP! Actually I was NPP before but I have realized they will not come and do anything so I am giving my vote to Kofi Bonzi," People's Man said.

"Ah don't waste something precious as your vote on a thief. What can Kofi Bonzi do? Let's bring NPP and Ghana would be better. Don't you want to come out of the heat wave blowing across the country?" the man inquired.

"Ghana would have been better long time ago if NPP could do it," People's Man uttered.

"What do you mean?" the man asked.

"I mean they have been in power before and still the country is the same, no change," People's Man explained.

"But do you expect anything better if NDC rules?" the customer demanded.

"And if NPP did anything better we would still be enjoying them despite the fact that NDC is ruling," People's Man said.

"No! NDC came to spoil every good thing NPP had done. Don't you understand?" the man queried.

"I understand," People's Man said calmly. "But my argument is if they did anything better like provided jobs and built factories, we would still have been enjoying them despite NDC being in power. Don't you see what Kwame Nkrumah did?"

"What do you mean?" the man asked.

"When good people rule their works transcend for years," People's Man explained. "Watch Ghana now, all the valuable things the country is running on were done by Nkrumah and that was about fifty something years ago. NPP was in power just fifteen years ago and tell me what they did that is still running and benefiting this country. Nothing. And when they come again, they are going to do nothing. They only want to be in power so they can get closer to the money and steal it like NDC is doing now. They are all the same, no difference. Ghanaians are only being deceived by their big English. Let's vote for visionaries like Kwame Nkrumah and Ghana would become better. I believe Kofi Bonzi stands tall among all the candidates running for Presidency this year. So let's try him.

After all we've been living with NPP and NDC all our lives and they have not helped. So what prevents us from trying someone else? Who knows, maybe things could be different." People's Man placed one pair of glittering shoe down and the man began to wear it.

"Hmm you've said something oo. Akosombo, Tema, Takoradi, schools and even more, all built by Kwame Nkrumah," the man admitted "How old are you?"

"Am twenty- four years old," People's Man answered. "I have finished senior high school and look at the job I am doing. In Nkrumah's days, I heard senior high school graduates got jobs before they even left school not to mention university graduates. Now in our modern Ghana there are university graduates who finished school before we began our fourth republic democracy and are still at home without jobs...."

"Am one of them," the man divulged. "Eighteen years now and I still have got no work that fits my level of education."

"Yet NPP and NDC have come and gone and NDC is here again," People's Man stressed "So what makes you think NPP can do anything when they also come back? Let's try someone else".

The other shoe came down, glittering as the sun's rays fell on it. The man wore his other half pair without any comment again. He took out ten cedis and gave it to People's Man. People's Man got up to find change for him.

"No keep the change," the man said with a smile. "I like the spirit with which you speak. Remember that inferior work is better than to steal. Take good care of yourself okay and keep away from bad company."

People's Man kept saying "...thank you, thank you...."

"Don't worry," the man said. "Today a twenty-four year old has convinced me to change my vote. I can't believe it. All I shall tell you is to keep the spirit."

The man was gone and People's Man picked his box and started drumming "...shine, shine, shine your shoes...."

He was starting the campaign again tonight, he decided. He could make impact if he kept the momentum.

12

People's Man was at the 'Pentagon' at exactly four in the evening. In the evenings, work was not good because people who had closed from work did not need their shoes shined. It was those going in the mornings that normally patronized. So work was good in the morning and early afternoons but slow in the evening and People's Man never wasted time wandering about.

He got to Oga Molu and threw in two APC bottles of Akpeteshie and grabbed two rolls of marijuana. Tonight he was going out to campaign and he had planned to say it all. He knew people were listening and that they would listen. It's been a while since his last campaign at the station and People's Man believed he could face the crowd if he threw in more Akpeteshie. He was going to attack everyone. Evening drinkers and smokers came in and went out. Occasionally, one or two would throw greetings at People's Man and he would respond.

As he sat, People's Man reminisced about the events of the day, how the sun had scorched him and the miles he had walked, all for just a little. And already, Oga Molu was eating into his little 'coin'. After smoking his two rolls of marijuana, People's Man got up and took two APC bottles more of Akpeteshie.

By the time he was stumbling out of the 'Pentagon', the crowd in the video room had started spewing out.

With his megaphone, People's Man entered the Odawna 'trotro' station at 6:10pm and immediately started his political preaching. People were trickling in, queues were forming and some cars were half full. The shouts of car mates could be heard here and there as they called for passengers. People's Man's megaphone sounded and the shouts of mates were swallowed up.

"Anuanom me kyea mo," he began. "I have come again for us to continue the conversation I had been having with you every day. Now we have only two months left and elections are coming on. I continue to urge you to prepare your minds and vote for Kofi Bonzi and OPP in both presidential and parliamentary ballots this year. We are embarking on 'operation removing NDC and forgetting NPP'. The party you should vote for is OPP.

"Let us all come together and make Kofi Bonzi President so that he can change this country for us. The last time, the President said Kofi Bonzi was a thief. It is the President and his people who are thieves. NDC and NPP are full of corrupt people. Over the years both have ruled but we are in the same situation.

"Nothing shows that they can do anything for this country. It is the same borrowing and borrowing everyday and they steal the money themselves. They only use a little to make shoddy works for us. Who is a thief more than people like these? Ghana, wake up! The suffering should come to an end. It is about time we moved forward. Now the children of Ghana have become a useless bunch and many are turning into drug addicts, armed robbers and prostitutes. We cannot sit down as a nation for this to happen to us. Let us start seeking for good leaders who could turn our fortunes around and forget about NPP and NDC...."

People's Man was heating up. The sweat had begun to pour and Akpeteshie was on a fast track. The chanting was reaching a crescendo. Then suddenly, two motor bikes with four macho men on them bumped into the station and screeched to a stop beside him. Two of the macho men, one from each bike got down and started beating People's Man mercilessly. One grabbed his megaphone from his hand and smashed it on the floor. The slaps rained on his face and blows rammed into his stomach, face, back and all. People's Man tried to fight back but it was of no use as the two muscular men, their biceps looking like timber logs, slapped him and kicked him. A crowd gathered round the scene and as they surged forward to help People's Man, the two macho men on the motor bikes took out guns and gave two warning shots. Every one backed away and the crowd scattered chaotically as each one dashed away for his or her dear life.

A blow caught People's Man in the face and he fell down with a big thud, his head hitting the concrete floor in the process. Blood gushed out. When his assailants saw the blood and People's Man lying lifeless on the ground, they mounted their motorbikes and drove off, shooting into the air as they sped off.

The crowd, seeing that the threat to their lives was gone, gathered again around People's Man. Two station masters organized a 'trotro' car and People's Man was placed into it. They drove him straight to the 37 military hospital where he was admitted at the intensive care unit.

13

News of the assault on People's Man was on every radio station across the country as journalists chased around to know what actually happened and who were responsible. On Okay FM's morning talk show, the host had called the NDC general secretary and he was pointing an accusing finger at NPP.

"… the boy was making things difficult for them," he said.

"Why do you say that?" the host asked.

"Because the boy was pulling away their supporters for Kofi Bonzi," he replied. "Already they know they will not win this year's elections and he was pulling away the little support they had by exposing their corrupt nature."

"But he did not leave the NDC too out. He had accused you people too of corruption and has called the President a thief. Some people believe that had made the NDC send people to beat him," the host said.

"As for us we haven't sent anyone," the NDC general secretary declined the statement. "It is the NPP that has macho men. Information has reached us that they are gathering macho men to form a vigilante group and now they are using them to beat anyone who makes things difficult for them. NDC's support is not shaken, we still have strong support due to our good works and we have already won this year's elections so why the rush to beat someone? It is the NPP. I will advise the boy's family to take the NPP to court."

"Ok, thank you, we shall talk later," the host said. "Let me call the NPP general secretary to listen to his side of the story."

When the NPP general secretary was called, he lamented on the comments made by his NDC counterpart. "…sometimes I just get sad at the way the NDC people do their politics," he said. "If things go on like this, it would be difficult for us as a nation to establish confidence in our quest to see law and order work in this country. Something serious like this has happened to a young man who is trying to exercise his right. Freedom of speech, a key component in our democracy, has been compromised and NDC without evidence, please listen very carefully, they don't have evidence but the secretary general is establishing emphatically that it was the NPP who sent the macho men. How can he say something like that when NPP as a party don't know where this is coming from? I think comments on issues like this must be backed with evidence of some nature. One cannot just get up and start accusing the NPP when the party doesn't know anything about what went on at the Odawna 'trotro' station.

"As I speak now, I personally don't know this guy in question or even heard of him until now. How can we organize macho men to go after someone we have no idea on? It is the NDC who have macho men. The NPP have concrete evidence to back our claim. We are not like the NDC people who just wake up and start talking. NPP have always got evidence to back what they say and I am saying it on authority that NDC have formed groups comprising of macho men to cause commotion and confusion in this upcoming elections and that is what they have started doing. It looks as if they are bent on maintaining power and the boy's campaign was affecting them".

"Is that so?" the host asked. "Why do you say People's Man's campaign was affecting the NDC?"

"Because they are in power and Ghanaians have witnessed the bad way they are governing this country," the general secretary of the NPP replied. "The people already are fed up with NDC and the boy's campaign was highlighting their bad deeds. Now people do not have water to drink, parents cannot pay school fees, pregnant women die every day due to the lack of better health care which has seen the collapse of our health insurance, the health insurance policy NPP brought and…."

"These people think we are children eh?" Oga Molu got angry and shouted out. "Macho men have attacked an innocent guy like this and both NDC and NPP are on it again with their blame games. If it is not any of them, then who sent these macho men?"

The 'Pentagon' which was packed to the brim as they listened to the issue concerning People's Man suddenly buzzed into action, each person trying to speak his mind.

"Now these people want to control us mafia style," one guy voiced out. "We are a free people who have a right to free speech but it looks as if these political figures want to sit on our freedom. First it was the beating and killing of journalists and now they are shifting it onto us, ordinary people trying to speak our minds. What at all has come into their minds, that we should let them rule us by force? From what is going on, it looks as if they want to use mafia style to control our democracy and that should not be allowed else they will put fear into us and we won't be able to talk though they don't do the right thing."

"But what are we doing Circle boys?" another guy asked. "This thing calls for a demonstration. We should not wait for even a second, for this is an attack on all of us. People's Man was fighting for our wellbeing. So if NPP and NDC want to silence him, then it means they don't want the betterment of society. They rather wish life would always be the way it is, they alone always on top and enjoying. Ghana is not going well and we should not be afraid to say it, macho men or no macho men. We should go out and express our dislike. People's Man is our friend, we must show some love."

 "Yes I support that…." Fire Service admitted as he threw in a glassful of Akpeteshie. "Chooboii!"

"Yeii!" All in the bar responded.

" Chooboii!"

" Yeii!"

The crowd became agitated and Oga Molu was the beneficiary of the day as everyone turned to his counter.

"Oga APC…."

" Oga one roll…."

"Oga Adonko…."

"Oga K20…."
"Oga fame ko…."
"Oga…."

In the end, information had gone round and Circle boys organized themselves for a demonstration. Within two hours a great hoard of people had gathered at Obra Spot. A Soloku group offered free service and the crowd, most of them driven by alcohol, marijuana and cocaine hit the street with ' samamo'. Accompanied by a brass band they matched to 37 military hospital chanting down NPP and NDC.
"Ya bre mo", "NPP and NDC mo ma yen ho nto yen", "Ghana is free, Freedom of speech is our right", "NPP, NDC go away", "We are fed up with NDC and NPP", were some of the writings on their placards, Wango Pingo writing most of them.

The circle police commander made an immediate call to the regional command the moment he got the information about the sudden turn of events.
"Some youths have gathered to demonstrate against the beating of their colleague at the Odawna station. It seems I don't have the men to control them and I request for backup sir. These are ghetto youths and there is likely to be acts of lawlessness. They are heading for 37 area".

The Accra regional command immediately phoned the army commander at Burma camp and asked for help. By the time the demonstrators reached 37 military hospital, the whole place was full of military men. Three armored cars and two water cannons were parked at the entrance of the hospital. The demonstrators themselves, an army in number, immediately blocked traffic upon their arrival. People sat in their cars frustratingly while at the same time, they were curious about the spectacle. Those in 'trotro' and taxi cabs started disembarking to walk past the demonstrators to take cars on the other side.

The soldiers who had been deployed were on high alert. Presently a warning shot had been fired and guns were pointed at the demonstrators who were forcing to enter the hospital to demand to see the welfare of People's Man. Akpeteshie, K20, Adonko, mafia, marijuana and cocaine driven souls would not understand why they should be prevented from entering the hospital premises. They started pushing forward unperturbed, facing the guns pointed at them. The soldiers started going back a foot at a time. The demonstrators were pushing for a reaction from them but this was a fragile situation and they had to make sure blood was not shed. The crowd kept coming. Finally, the water cannons opened up and teargas was released. The crowd ran helter-skelter.

Angry by the actions of the soldiers, some of the boys began to throw stones. Rubber bullets were introduced and people fell as they were caught on the wrong side of their bodies. By the time the crowd was dispersed, there were twenty five injuries made up of three security men and twenty-two civilians. That notwithstanding sixty cars had their wind screens and side glasses smashed. The security service on the other hand saw the arrest of a hundred and fifty people.

The next day, the President asked for the release of all the arrested youths. He offered to pay compensations to people whose properties were affected and pay the hospital bills of those injured. The opposition NPP accused the President of taking advantage of the situation to score political points.

Kofi Bonzi of OPP condemned the actions that led to the happening of "... all these" calling it " ... unfortunate" and " ... unacceptable in a country that had practiced democracy for almost thirty years...."

He offered to pay all the hospital bills for People's Man who was reported on radio and T.V had fallen into a coma.

Press conferences had become the new norm in the country and any group with a following could just wake up and organize a press conference which hungry- for- news journalists were always ready to attend and cover. Currently, Oga Molu, the man who was arrested for being the leader of the ghetto demonstrators, had organized a press conference at Obra Spot. All the ghetto boys were there and many media houses had representatives there to cover.

Oga stood on the makeshift platform surrounded by journalists with recording gadgets while the ghetto youths sang 'samamo' and danced.

"...today this press conference has been organized to inform all ghetto boys all over the country to give their votes to Kofi Bonzi and OPP in the upcoming elections. People's Man was a ghetto boy and it was his dream to fight and see a better life for all ghetto youths who have been neglected to their fate and are left without hope in this country because of bad governance and greediness. We are fed up with the rule of NPP and NDC and if you are a ghetto man and you are listening, we all are coming together across the country to support OPP and Kofi Bonzi .... He is the one who can...."

By the time the press conference which some radio stations broadcasted live was over, it was trending on social media that ghetto boys at 'New York' and 'Main Spain' in Takoradi had joined the revolution. In the days that followed, ghetto youths at 'Tinka' in Kumasi joined and those at Tarkwa 'Pump side' also gave their support. Then there were reports that Central region and other regions were joining the support for Kofi Bonzi and his OPP.

Many Ghanaians who heard the full story and the reason why People's Man had fallen into coma also gave their support. The NPP and NDC were getting out of hand. In an era of democracy, these people were still using intimidation and force to control the country to their advantage, something almost similar to the military rule the country experienced decades ago. This was unacceptable. People's Man's case was the peak of many that had seen the deaths of political party members and journalists. The use of violence to keep people from expressing themselves was on the rise and many Ghanaians, who knew NPP and NDC were responsible for many of this violence, were getting fed up. All these people were planning to vote for Kofi Bonzi.

When People's Man woke up he was at first seeing things in hazy outlines but as the days wore on, he edged towards convalescence until he could get up and shower on his own. His whole skull was in bandage and talking was a little difficult. One day, he had finished showering, finished his breakfast and was preparing for medication when he had a surprise visit.

Kofi Bonzi, flanked by OPP leaders, came into his ward and sat around his bed with Kofi Bonzi close beside him. People's Man though hurt, was filled with a kind of elation words could not express. Sometimes bad situations could lead to good things. All his days in Accra, he had to hustle in the sun to make ends meet. But as People's Man reclined on his bed surrounded by the big men of OPP, he knew that the hustle was going to come to an end. Finally, life could change for the better. Kofi Bonzi talked to him with assurances and gave him his business card saying, "...call me the moment you are discharged and I will come for you okay?"

People's Man nodded. Kofi Bonzi gave him a bundle of twenty cedi notes together with a lot of gifts and bid him farewell.

As Kofi Bonzi's car drove out of the hospital's compound, he was contemplating getting People's Man on his campaign train to attract sympathy votes. Things were getting better and prospects were brighter every passing day.

16

The few weeks before elections had been very hot and exciting. Campaigning by the political parties intensified with NDC and NPP doubling their efforts because almost the whole country was throwing their support for Kofi Bonzi and defeat was staring them in the face.

The NDC, which was the party in power, had started fresh and emergency projects in constituencies considered their strongholds. Roads were being asphalted, gutters constructed, community centers and toilets were being built, boreholes were being dug overnight and people were receiving gifts and money. Life in a short time was getting better in these constituencies. Meanwhile, just some few years back government had dragged its feet to requests by these same communities to have their infrastructure and amenities fixed. NPP accused the ruling NDC of hypocrisy and vote buying, while OPP and other smaller parties used the sudden increase in the construction of infrastructure to back their argument that money was there but it was not being put to good use. They cautioned Ghanaians to be careful of deceit because after elections no projects will come again and the ones being done will be abandoned.

A week before elections Kofi Bonzi and his Other People's Party organized a big rally at Takoradi, his own backyard. And there, he told a story of a ghetto boy struggling to make life in a country where corrupt people rule and where money for the people were diverted into private pockets leaving people like People's Man to suffer bad fate, a fate forced on them by greedy men whose modus operandi was deceit. But he urged Ghanaians not to be deceived anymore.

With People's Man standing by his side he said "…we have come a long way and many years and many struggles could only make fools wise, the loyal rebellious and the blind in mind enlightened. This election is a fight for our freedom, a freedom compromised by greedy men whose motives were evil. Like vampires, these greedy men are sucking away the people's blood through corruption, greed and intimidation.

"I myself have been a ghetto boy before at 'New York' and from there managed to run out of this country. Outside, I saw a change in my life, a change that would not have happened if I had remained in this country. In Ghana today, life is a struggle, people stumble and fall in a quest to escape hardship like this young man with me here whose quest to change his life was met with violence. And this violence was visited upon him by the people who rule all because these people, NPP and NDC, want to lay a heavy hand on this country. Meanwhile, there is nothing they could do and have done for our dear nation. We are a free people and it is our responsibility to guard our freedom.

"With NPP and NDC, Ghana is in bondage and we can only escape from this bondage if we vote wisely. Vote OPP, vote for me because I understand your problems, our problems and I am prepared to help you solve them. The future is bright but we shall not see this brightness if we continue to keep NPP and NDC. OPP!"

"Yeah you know me," the rally grounds vibrated.

After the rally, many radio and T.V stations granted People's Man interviews. And this happened everywhere Kofi Bonzi had a rally. People's Man's messages were now reaching a wide range of Ghanaians, wider than he had reached at Circle Odawna 'trotro' station.

17

The day of elections finally arrived and Ghanaians as usual did it again. Prior to the day of balloting the country had looked as though civil war was coming as the political parties debated their course and each fought to have their messages reach the people. It was a real wrangle and the atmosphere, as electrified and agitated as had been, ironically became calm on elections day.

It was so in Ghana and as the country's democracy grew stronger and stronger, the wrangling, fusing and heated debates that characterized election years became less a concern to citizens who knew and understood politics and had developed a tolerance for each other to the extent that it was beautiful to see how people queued calmly to cast their vote. Ghana's year of elections was like a volcano, when it erupts you'd never think it will sleep.

Many things had gone on concurrently as the final day approached. NPP had finally made NDC's meeting about causing 'confusion' public. They had positioned informants at the various borders not only with Togo but with Burkina Faso and Cote d'ivoire. Vigilante macho men were at every polling station in case the NDC macho men came and they made this also public.
NDC on the other hand saw a lot of confusion going on in its strongholds and other areas where they wanted to capture.

Gifts and items meant for voters were hijacked by constituency executives and assembly men and the very people who would vote for the party were ignored. Money meant for macho men were compromised and this caused anger with the macho men threatening to disobey instructions because they were not fools to waste their lives for people who never cared about their welfare. Projects that had erupted suddenly in the constituencies were being slowed and this was the plans of D.C.Es and M.C.Es to keep the money for themselves. Meanwhile discerning members in these constituencies judged their plans and made decisions on their own. One of these decisions was to vote 'skirt and blouse'.

So in the end the 'coffin and corpse' from Togo never came and ballot boxes never went anywhere. All these worked to the advantage of Kofi Bonzi who smaller parties like GUM, CPP and APC had dedicated their support and urged all followers to vote for.

By five o'clock in the evening when voting finally came to a close, only one or two unfortunate incidents had been recorded by the police who had been very vigilant and hardworking. This was because the NDC tape NPP brought out had implicated them of taking bribes. Counting finally began and throughout the night dedicated journalists worked to bring the results of the elections to waiting Ghanaians who glued to their radios and televisions. Occasionally, shouts and jubilations erupted across the land as OPP and their presidential candidate Kofi Bonzi, hijacked strongholds of NPP and NDC.

18

The Electoral Commissioner called a press conference to finally declare the winner of the elections. His face as was his nature was very calm. Yet within him he was a very happy man. He had overseen six elections and if it were not by the grace of God and his strong heart, the combined pressure from NPP and NDC alone would have made him a dead man by now. Of these six elections he had conducted for the country, both NDC and NPP had emerged winners. Yet any time one of these parties found themselves in opposition, the Electoral Commissioner became an enemy. If NDC loses power they accuse the commission of helping NPP and if NPP loses power, they also accuse the commission of helping NDC. He had anticipated a similar blame game in these elections but thank God NPP and NDC came nowhere near to winning. He was very happy. For once he was going to announce the results of an election and go home to sleep in peace.

He smirked before he began, "… twelve million four hundred and three thousand people voted in this year's elections. Of this number, NPP had two million, five hundred and twenty one thousand, representing 20.4% of total vote cast. NDC had three million, one hundred and thirty six thousand, representing 25.3% of the total vote cast and OPP had six million seven hundred and forty six thousand representing 54.3% of total vote cast. Patently, from the declaration of the results, I stand in the power vested in me to announce that, Kofi Bonzi, of the

OPP, is the newly elected President of the republic of Ghana." After the announcement, he closed his files and gathered his papers to leave.

Outside, the whole country erupted into jubilation. Brass bands immediately came out, gigantic speakers were mounted on streets and music flowed, 'Soloku' struck the streets and the ladies gave their big buttocks to the guys to fondle for free. Happiness was in the air and a new atmosphere of hope erupted everywhere.

19

Kofi Bonzi was now the President and People's Man was with him. It travelled all around Circle that People's Man was the President's best man and rode in his convoy wherever he went. All assumed People's Man was lucky and happy. Some of the ghetto boys envied him, though.

The President had formed an all-inclusive government bringing in knowledgeable people from other political parties to participate in his governance. This was a move many praised him for because one party could not have all the big brains the country needed in other to move forward.

However after a year and a half of his rule, Ghanaians started getting disappointed in Kofi Bonzi and People's Man was not left out. He did not know what was going on. Wasn't this the Kofi Bonzi who had promised Ghanaians all the good things? And yet fuel prices were rising, bad roads had not been fixed and the few good ones were degrading. Electricity bills were rising and the power itself was not reliable. Taxes have been increased and traders and consumers were complaining vehemently, transport fares were going up and cost of living kept rising. Farmers were crying, market women were wincing and people cried for money and jobs. Even his much talked about dustbins had not arrived and the cities were getting even dirtier. Odawna River continued to stink and it still maintained its status as 'the disgrace of the city'.

Nothing new seems to be going on inside Kofi Bonzi's government. Just the normal running of government business - giving money to the ministers to take care of their sectors, collecting taxes to finance government machinery and when this was not enough, he resorted to borrowing to support the budget. No innovations, nothing new, no bold initiatives that can bring good jobs on a massive scale to lift the fortunes of the people who had placed their hope in the OPP.

One afternoon, People's Man had been called to the President's office. There, he met some of the big men of Other People's Party sitting with the President. People's Man was given a seat on the President's right hand. As he sat down, the President patted him lightly on the shoulder.

"People's Man," he looked at the President. "I have called you in here this afternoon to reward you for the hard work you did to help bring my party to power. In fact I am very appreciative and today I am rewarding all party members who did well to bring us into power. You did a good job. It had taken a while to do this because the finance minister had some financial constraints and it's until now that he had released the amount I asked him for. Brefo come here!" The president called his bodyguard who was standing behind him all these while. The bodyguard stepped forward.

"Pick those envelops on the table and share among them, one for each person," the President commanded.

The body guard picked the envelops and shared them among those gathered inside the office save the President.

When he had finished, the President said "Inside each envelop is a check and its quite satisfactory," he turned to People's Man "you can buy a house or build one and also get a car, then you can do whatever you like with the rest. You have been a blessing to my course and I will never forget you."

People's Man held his envelop in his hand. The others in the room opened their own and started smiling when they saw the fat check inside. After a minute or so, People's Man got up and placed his envelop back on the table.

"Mo Ghana mpaninfo paa enti saa na mo suban te?" he turned to the President, "Mr. President , people placed their hopes in you, ignored the incompetent NPP and NDC and voted for you to become President at first trial, something unprecedented in this country and you sit here sharing money without caring about what Ghanaians are going through?"

One of the OPP leaders who was also a cabinet minister gestured to talk but the President raised his hand to stop him.

"People's Man the problems of Ghanaians will be solved, but it is not an overnight thing to do. It takes time. We shall get to them," the President said calmly.

"Mr. President you had talked big and made the people's problems small. They had trust in you and it will be unfair to rule this way. Now you seem to have forgotten all your promises."

"I haven't forgotten them People's Man. We shall do everything we said but I must be frank it's not everything we can do," the President divulged.

"Then why did you tell the people you could do them Mr. President?" People's Man asked.

"Oh my boy, that is politics. If you don't tell them that they will not vote for you. In politics you learn how to care on stage but when reality dawns on you, you give them what you can find. In politics we don't walk the talk. The doing takes time and some are not even feasible in a third world country like our own."

"Oh Mr. President, in fact you disappoint me," People's Man berated. "Truly, you have disappointed me dearly. So when are we going to find a savior for our country? Many of you come from deprived places but when you get into the seat of government you forget the people who made you. All you begin to think of are your selfish gains. You are a bunch of greedy men. I regret laying down my life for greedy people like you. The welfare of the ordinary Ghanaian is not important to you one bit. You give them lies, they give you power and you grab what you want and forget them. This is wickedness.

"Get out there and see how many Ghanaian youths are turning into drug addicts, ghetto boys and armed robbers while young ladies are turning into prostitution as a means of survival all because there are no jobs for them to do. Get out there and see how women hustle in the scorching sun in the various markets across the country in order to feed their families. Go out there and see how many marriages are breaking up because of financial problems. Go out there and see how pregnant women are dying at child birth.

"Go out there and see how malaria, common malaria sickness, a sickness highly controllable, is killing hundreds because of poorly constructed drains, unclean environment, poor nutrition and the lack of money to buy drugs. And you sit here sharing money?

"Go out there and see how the Ghanaian farmer is suffering before he could produce for this nation to get food to eat. Go out there and see how many had become mentally deranged because of poverty."

People's Man was on his feet now and was facing the President directly. The body guard tried to pull him down to his seat but the President's hand came up and he stopped. People's Man had tears gathered in his eyes and now a drop trickled down.

"How come other countries have made it?" he asked. "How come they have been able to develop and their citizens are enjoying life? Are they more human than us?

"South Africa with its gold deposit had turned their fortunes around, Saudi Arabia with their oil is doing well for its people, Britain with their human resource and good thinking is ruling the financial world, Russia with oil and gas is a super power and with their huge population China is ruling the commercial world. Ghana has gold, diamond, bauxite, manganese, a huge forest, land, rain, sun and now oil and gas and still the country is sinking every day.

"Sometimes are you people not ashamed to be the leaders of a country like this and yet its citizens are still suffering? It's a disgrace to our leaders. Compared to other leaders of the world, we African youths are ashamed of our leaders. It is like they have inferior minds. It's like our leaders cannot think. A bunch of timid minded souls who can only devise means of stealing their country's money instead of making them a better one. You turned to politics because of money and selfish gains. You use our country as collateral to take big loans and share. When your time is up you will go without caring what happens next. Aren't you ashamed when after sixty something years only Kwame Nkrumah's name is mentioned everyday as the only wisest man Africa has had. What is wrong with all the schooling, all the education you have attained? Are all those big certificates meant to steal our monies? Shameful, I will not be part of this. I'm out. I joined politics to see a change. A change for the people, those I am with at the ghetto and those suffering because of the evil that goes on every day. Get out there and see how many people die every day trying to cross the desert to find good living in western countries. Fire burn you all." And People's Man walked to the door of the office and was gone.

When People's Man left, one of the OPP members said, "But Mr. President this small chap cannot speak to us like he did. I think he should be…."

"Leave him alone," the President said and got up. "I understand him."

When People's Man entered the 'Pentagon' the few smokers who sat whiling away the hot afternoon immediately shouted his name and all of them stood up to hug him. Within minutes words went around that People's Man had arrived and all his friends in the Circle area trooped into the 'Pentagon' to see him. Those inside the video room immediately poured out leaving the movies unwatched and People's Man was suddenly surrounded by a hoard of ghetto youths in a short time. And as People's Man watched them touch him and ask him about life at the Jubilee House, he became extremely sad.

These were his friends, the children of Ghana and they looked like a brood of chicken without a mother, a people without direction, their destinies locked at the ghetto with no sign of hope. He recognized a few who were his close friends and they had lived life together when he was at the ghetto. Osama, his beard left unkempt was holding a big bundle of marijuana roll and he smiled when their eyes met revealing a set of brown smoke stained teeth. Hero, had a big chain with a cross at the end around his neck, across the bar of the cross was written 'Rick Ross'. Soobolo, the cocaine boy, looked thin and white yet he was beaming with smiles as he watched People's Man. 50 Cent was disheveled and it looked as if he was turning his bushy hair into dreadlocks. Isha, still looking beautiful, was wearing a pair of shorts which was pulled bellow her buttocks in 'Otto Pfister' style. Some had their shirts removed to cool their bodies in the afternoon heat and their ribs could be counted ending with protruding shoulder blades which many referred to as 'Rawlings' chain'.

Standing among them, People's Man realized how he had changed within these few months he had spent around the President. His skin had become smooth, his lips reddening and he looked more like a gentleman rather than a ghetto boy. Life really was good somewhere he thought, as the good meals and drinks flashed through his mind. Even the food that ended in the garbage at the Jubilee House could be a delicacy for these hungry fellows. They watched People's Man, expecting him to tell them something good, something reassuring coming from the Presidency for the ghetto boys. But all that he could do was stand quietly and as his heart felt heavy, he found his way through the thick crowd and with the money he had saved while he hung around the President, asked Oga Molu to give everyone what they wanted. Then he himself gulped down two APC bottles of Akpeteshie, the hot drink tearing his inner being as it descended down his torso. The people rejoiced and asked Oga to play music for them to party.

People's Man was back, at least one of them was representing at the Presidency and this called for a celebration. Oga opened the volume of the music high.

'Bhim……' the huge speakers sounded.

"Heiiii…" The crowd shouted and they started dancing. The party had begun. Oga Molu was overwhelmed as people requested for their drinks.

"Oga Adonko six tots…."
"Oga K20 eight…."
"Oga two rolls …."
"Oga Guinness…."
"Oga Club…."
"Oga APC…."
"Oga three rolls…."
"Oga fame ko…"
"Oga…., Oga…, Oga…."

In the days that followed, everyone expected People's Man to return to the Jubilee House but he remained with them. He now shared his little kiosk with Gordon, the guy from his hometown who had thought the kiosk had become his when People's Man left. Days ran into weeks and weeks into months and still People's Man was with them. He was now drinking the Akpeteshie with them, smoking the weed with them and hanged about aimlessly like them. When the heat caught up with him, People's Man picked his shoeshine box and started the hustling once more. All these while he had not told anyone what had brought him back to the ghetto. As he passed, he could feel groups discussing him and others pointed in his direction and spoke in hushed tones.

When they waited and People's Man was not telling them anything concerning his comeback, the ghetto youths began to make their own stories. Some said People's Man had gone to do some 'nkurasesem' at the Jubilee House and the President had sacked him. Others said the Other People's Party had used People's Man like the way NPP and NDC used the ghetto youths and dumped them. On the lighter side, others teased him saying he had stolen the President's meat and the President had said People's Man was a hungry dog and turned him away.

When People's man did something that pissed someone off, they will tell him to 'fuck off' and add 'Kuraseni'. In the midst of all these, People's Man never spoke a word as he nursed his grief alone. To him, any word from his mouth was going to expose the President and bring him down. Yet People's Man saw Kofi Bonzi as his making and it pained his heart to raze down something he himself had built, something as beautiful as helping to make someone the president. Bringing Kofi Bonzi down was like bringing his own self down. All along there was one person People's Man was looking for to share his story with and that was Wango Pingo. Wango was not patronizing the 'Pentagon' anymore and no one could tell him why.

One afternoon, as People's Man walked a part of the city drumming on his box to call customers, he saw Wango in his car caught up in a traffic jam.
"Doctor Wango!" he shouted.
"People's Man!" Wango Pingo who looked visibly shocked, asked People's Man to join him in his car.

With his shoeshine box, People's Man embarked and sat beside Wango in the front passenger seat.

"But why this?" Wango pointed at the shoeshine box.

"Oh Doctor I have been looking for you oo."

People's Man narrated all that had transpired and ended up saying "...Doctor I could not think of me becoming rich overnight while the people I fought for remained in their suffering and poverty. No I just could not so…."

"So you left the fat cheque right?" Wango asked calmly.

"Yes".

"That was a mistake. You should have taken the money. It's Ghana's money and you deserve it too," Wango said.

"But Doctor …."

"I understand you," Wango said assuring "I understand you. Have you told anyone?" he asked.

"No," People's Man answered.

"Okay don't tell anyone else they will say you are 'otolegey'," Wango cautioned. "They will say you are foolish but I understand you. I will only tell you to continue with that spirit of loyalty and God himself will reward you. And don't worry; you know I kept telling you they are all the same. I don't know if it's a curse on Africa. They are all the same, from the south to the north not leaving the east and the west. But you don't worry and don't tell anyone."

"But why are you not coming to the 'Pentagon' Doctor?" People's Man asked.

"Don't mind that greedy man," referring to Oga Molu. "When you were at the hospital we had organized a demonstration. And when the political parties saw that we were pulling the ghetto boys for Kofi Bonzi, they started bringing in money to keep our mouths shut. Can you imagine Oga alone kept the money and never gave some to anyone? NPP brought money, NDC brought money and OPP brought money, big money to keep him talking. He never gave anyone some though we all fought for this course. He is greedy like your man," Wango said.

"Hmm," People's Man sighed.

Wango gave People's Man money and told him to stay strong.

21

He beamed with smiles but the old woman looked sad. As he got closer he saw her crying, then she stretched her hand and said 'I am hungry'. Suddenly her crying became hysteric and he saw blood oozing from every hole around her head. Blood poured from her eyes, blood poured from her ears and finally when she opened her mouth to talk again blood gushed out of her mouth like water from a fountain. Suddenly he was soaked in blood from head to toe. When he tried to help, the old woman turned into a monster and began to chase him. He gestured to run but his legs were heavy and they could not carry him faster. The monster closed up and was going to grab him….

He woke up with a start and sat on the bed. As he groped around to find the bedside lamp, he kept thanking God that the nightmare was only a dream. It was so real he could still feel the fear trapped in him. The bedside lamp came on and he took a look around. All was well. It was only a dream. He laid supine on the bed again, adjusted a pillow under his head and delved into his imaginations trying to reconstruct what he saw – the bad dream, the nightmare. It looked as if he knew the old woman he had seen in the dream somewhere. He was so sure. He contemplated, going deeper and deeper into his brain until he remembered. It was that old woman who had invited him into her house.

His campaign train had hit an area in the Brong and Ahafo region and somewhere near Brekum he had entered a small village for a short rally. As he stood talking to the people, some elders of the town had come to him with a bottle of schnapp and some cowries and told him the oldest woman in the village have asked to see him. Kofi Bonzi had accepted the invitation and had gone with the elders immediately. The old woman sat in a chair and from what he saw, she looked like she was blind but she mentioned his name the moment he entered the hall which surprisingly looked well decorated.

"Kofi," she said. "You are blessed."

"Amen," Kofi Bonzi who needed a spiritual intervention that time responded.

"My name is Lucy, yes Akosua Lucy," she began, "I am a hundred and three years old and if you go round they will tell you I am the oldest woman in this town. All my life I have lived in Europe, Holland to be precise and there, I was a seer. I told people their fortunes for a living. When I was getting old, I decided to finally come home and stay with my family. But here I don't practice soothsaying because they will say I am a witch although I still see the ground. I knew you were coming and I have a message for you". She took a handkerchief and cleared her nose. "When I lived in Ghana in the sixties, I saw how Kwame Nkrumah ran this country," she continued. "Ghana had everything. But the moment they overthrew Nkrumah life became very hard for us and many of us travelled to Europe and America. Living in Europe, I saw how they had built a system that made life better and easy for their citizens. It was just like what Kwame Nkrumah was doing for this country and the rest of Africa. For a long time I have been looking to see who can rise to become like him but all over the years there had been none like him. Yet today, when you stepped here, I was told you are the one who will turn this country's fortunes around so I have called you here to bless you.

"This country has got everything, yet the children are suffering. When you become president, which you would, try and turn their fortunes around for good. All this country needs is good and loyal people to lead it. Be careful to stay focused and don't be afraid of anything because you are the chosen one. And also look out for the guardian for he will come and when he comes listen to him...."

She had held out her hands to Kofi Bonzi who grabbed them and she prayed for him. When he came out, he never knew the crowd had followed him to the house. They lifted him into the air and shouted "...abrewa akasa oo abrewa akasa....". They hailed him as the next President because the people said, that old woman had powerful words and everything she said came to pass. And once she called him, the people concluded he was the next president.

Truly, he had won the elections and truly, he had become the President but why such a horrible dream this night? The old woman had asked him to help the people. And was he doing so? He asked himself while lying supine on his bed.

Presently he thought of what had pushed him to run for the presidency. As a businessman seeking more investments, he had heard most of the oil companies who mined Ghana's crude oil were moving out and their shares were being sold to other companies. His oil company had put in a bid but the NDC government was bent on giving the concession to different companies which belonged to foreign nationals. To get the concession which he needed so badly, he decided to make sure he grabbed power. So he had opted to try and see if it could be possible and it turned positive for him. Now his company had succeeded in grabbing everything and Ghana's oil industry was now in his hands. Mission accomplished. But was that fair? He asked himself. He himself had lived in Ghana before he had run away to the United States of America. He knew how hard it was to make a living in the country and these people some hungry, some poor, some sick with all hopes fading, had come together to put their trust in him. Yet he was riding on their votes to reach his dreams and had ignored them. Now most of the promises he gave them have been thrown somewhere and though few ones had been accomplished, compared to previous governments he had done little. The people had started comparing him to the previous NDC government which was in power and he knew he was losing grounds. There were difficulties in the health sector, inflation was rising, taxes had to be increased to make more money which was needed to run the economy, the cities and towns were still dirty and his much talked about dustbins had not even been deployed. Things were still going the old way and were even getting worse. News from the ground was not good as people complained everyday of hardship.

Now if he failed to do anything for them, would these people ever trust any political party again apart from NPP and NDC? No! He has to instill confidence in the people and make them believe they can trust someone; else the country's democracy could suffer a setback. What at all was he grabbing all the money for? People were hungry, people were sick, hopes were lost and he amassed wealth that could feed millions and help thousands to make their lives better. Even at that, he was not supposed to do all these with his money but the people's money, the country's money. Why then was he not helping them? He had left everything in the care of his ministers who were on a corruption spree. Information had reached him about how the people in his government were amassing the country's wealth for themselves. Money meant for projects were being diverted into private accounts and his policies were not reaching the ground. The people were seeing nothing from him and he was getting unpopular. Meanwhile his grandmother had once told him that '…good name is better than riches….'

NPP and NDC were a failure and after him, he did not know who else would help this country. He understood their sufferings, he understood their pain, and he understood the pangs they went through because he had been there before.
He suddenly sat up on his bed. Things must change. He must be committed. Ghana must see a change under his rule. A change

for the better. The old woman had said a guardian would come. And where is that guardian? He needed someone to help him do this. Someone with the kind of love and commitment he has now got for the country. Someone who could be truthful and who he can trust and count on. His ministers were failing. They were all a greedy bunch and if he did not take care their greed will expose him and disgrace him. He needed a senior minister whose duty would be to monitor all the other ministers to make sure they do the right thing and also monitor corruption. It was about time he prosecuted corrupt public officials to save millions for development.

He needed someone loyal, someone truthful, someone with a love for the country, someone who would expose corruption and hold his ministers in check, someone…. His mind roamed, someone, someone, some… People's Man. The name jumped into his brain. Then he remembered, '…the guardian would come….' the old woman had said. When she said that OPP was already formed and no one had joined them again except…. Then he remembered again, People's Man's name came on the radio that night when reporters reported of a young man who had been hurt because he was campaigning for him. He had gone for People's Man and things had changed. The people's support for him rocketed, ghetto boys decided the outcome of the elections and he had won. The Guardian. People's Man too had talked about Kwame Nkrumah. On his campaign tour across the country he saw how the old Ghana had been raised. A look around revealed old factories and projects and though some of these factories were rotten away, they told the story of a big dream and how Ghana rose from the beginning. It was big. All the projects of Nkrumah spoke for themselves. The beginning was great and his works showed it just like the skeleton of a dinosaur showed how a gigantic mammal had once lived on earth. Many years and these skeletons were gradually rotting off and just like an archeologist, someone needed to dig these skeletons and keep them for preservation so that posterity could see the beauty of the past, a past that still lived like the skeleton of a dinosaur in a museum.

And as much as archeologists cannot bring a dinosaur to life by the mere presence of its skeletons, it was different with dreams. Dreams could be revived, dreams were immortal and though people die, their dreams could live into the future depending on who became the custodians of these dreams. People had dreams to build airplanes but they died before their dreams could materialize. Yet we have planes flying around today, some as big as the skies. Many dreams had survived without the dreamers because visionaries picked up these dreams and pursued them. People's Man, the guardian, People's Man, the senior minister. He would take the chap to university else these ministers would outmaneuver him. He was the only one with the spirit of loyalty and that was what he needed right now for his government to perform.

The President got up and walked to his bedroom door. The moment he opened the door, the bodyguard still on attention, saluted.

"Who is the commander on duty Tanko?" the President asked.

"Captain Duah sir"

"Call him for me."

The captain was around within a few minutes. He met the President sitting in a sofa.

"Do you know People's Man captain?" he asked. "That young man who was walking around here sometime ago. I hope you remember him?"

"Yes sir."

"Go and get him for me immediately, use my car," the President instructed.

"Yes sir."

22

People's Man watched the glassful of Akpeteshie for a while before he picked the drink and tossed it into his mouth. The usual sighing and face making followed, then he took his roll of marijuana from Oga, paid him – Oga was not crediting him anymore - and took a seat to smoke. He was smoking and was travelling in his head, thinking of how to survive the day when Gordon his roommate came in running to him.

"People's Man soldiers are looking for you run!" he said, panting.

"What have I done?" People's Man asked.

"I don't know they are all around," Gordon divulged.

"Maybe it is a 'scatter'," Oga Molu guessed. "Hey Rocky come take the stuff away!"

"No, they are asking for People's Man," Gordon affirmed.

People's Man threw away the marijuana in his hand. Now crime-free, he walked out to face the soldiers for he knew he had not committed any crime.

Gordon followed, so did Oga, Rocky and all those who were at the 'Pentagon' this early morning.

When People's Man reached where his kiosk was standing he saw the fleet of cars and motorbikes which filled the air with their sirens. All these were parked on the street ahead.

Captain Duah who People's Man recognized at once stepped forward and extended a hand. People's Man shook his hand.

"People's Man the President requests for you immediately so get into the car and let's go," the captain said.

"Captain what have I done?" People's Man humbly asked.

"I don't think there is any trouble but whatever it is I think it's urgent."

People's Man followed the captain and embarked the President's car, the door held open by captain Duah. Then the convoy started moving, sirens flowing and People's Man was whisked away to the Jubilee House.

The big crowd that had gathered by now marveled and cheered as People's Man was carried away. Many were in tears, while yet many said "…it is because another elections are getting close. In times like that they know even the mad man…."

Isha took a look at her friend standing beside her and said, "Eii God works in mysterious ways."